THE
PRINCE OF ENGLAND

PRINCE HARRY AND HIS JOURNEY TO COCOS (KEELING) ISLANDS

NICHOLAS ARMSTRONG JR

MAPLE
PUBLISHERS

THE PRINCE OF ENGLAND

Author: NICHOLAS ARMSTRONG JR

Copyright © NICHOLAS ARMSTRONG JR (2025)

The right of NICHOLAS ARMSTRONG JR to be identified as author of this work has been asserted by the author in accordance with section 77 and 78 of the Copyright, Designs and Patents Act 1988.

First Published in 2025

ISBN 978-1-83538-563-0 (Paperback)
       978-1-83538-564-7 (Hardback)
       978-1-83538-565-4 (E-Book)

Book cover design and Book layout by:
       White Magic Studios
       www.whitemagicstudios.co.uk

Published by:
       Maple Publishers
       Fairbourne Drive, Atterbury,
       Milton Keynes,
       MK10 9RG, UK
       www.maplepublishers.com

CONTENTS

CHAPTER 1

The Lion of Judah and His Journey to England

I am Harry. I am the prince of England. I was inside my royal palace. I had a dream. In my dream I saw someone. I saw a former friend. I saw the lion of Judah. I saw Leo. I saw him outside my royal palace. I was sitting on my father's Golden kingship stool. I heard someone's voice. I stood upwards. I walked forward. I was in front of my white gates. I saw something. I saw something happening. I saw something strange. I saw something strange happening. I saw my royal white gates. I saw the gates opening. I saw the gates opening faster. I saw the gates of my father's castle. I saw the gates opening faster than a warrior. I walked through the gates. I was in front of my white royal gates. I saw something. I saw something happening. I saw something strange. I saw something strange happening. I saw my white royal gates closing. I saw my white royal gates closing faster. I saw my white royal gates closing faster than a pirate warrior. I looked downwards. I saw millions of lions. I saw someone. I saw a former friend. I saw someone walking forward. I saw the lion of Judah. I saw Leo. I saw him walking forward. I saw him climbing my father's royal castle. I saw him in front of me. I heard him telling me a story. I heard him telling me about a battle. I heard him telling me about battle between two nations. I heard him telling me about a war. I heard him telling me about a war between two nations. I heard the lion of Judah. I heard him commanding. I heard him commanding the prince of England. I heard him commanding me. I heard him commanding me to travel towards somewhere. I heard him commanding me for a mysterious journey. I heard him commanding me for peace, unity and freedom. I looked at the lion of Judah. I welcomed the lion of Judah. I saluted the lion of Judah. I agreed to his commands. I accepted his commands. I saw the lion of Judah. I saw him blessing the prince of England. I saw him blessing Prince Harry. I saw him blessing me. I looked at the lion of Judah. I saw him mentioning the Lord's prayer. I saw the lion of Judah. I saw him waving prayers. I saw him waving me goodbye. I saw him turning around. I saw him walking downwards. I saw him leaving my royal gates. I saw him walking downwards. I saw millions of lions. I saw the lion of Judah. I saw Leo. I saw him walking forward. I saw millions of lions looking at him. I saw millions of lions giving him walking space. I saw him walking. I saw him walking forward. I saw his lion armies. I saw them following him. I saw them following the king of Judah. I saw them following Leo. I saw them following him to their heavenly kingdom.

CHAPTER 2

Prince Harry and His Journey From England to Finland

I was sleeping on my father's kingship bed. I had a mysterious dream. I woke up suddenly. I was in happiness. I remembered something. I remembered my mysterious dream. I remembered a commandment. I decided to travel from England to a farther world. I decided to travel on a mysterious journey. I decided to travel from England to Cocos Keeling Islands. I decided to travel for peace, unity and freedom. I decided to travel in order to bring peace, unity and freedom for two war nations. I jumped off my father's kingship bed. I walked forward. I turned around. I saw my red wardrobe. I went inside my red wardrobe. I searched for my red garments. I found my heavy red garments. I wore my heavy red garments. I turned around. I walked forward. I walked outside my red wardrobe. I walked forward. I walked towards another wardrobe. I walked towards a white wardrobe. I went inside my white wardrobe. I searched for something. I searched for something protective. I searched for my red and white armours. I searched for my red and white protective armours. I founded my red and white protective armours. I turned around. I walked forward. I walked outside my white wardrobe. I turned around. I walked forward. I threw my red garments on my father's kingship bed. I placed my red and white protective armours on the floor. I wore my red garments. I placed my red and white protected armours on my shoulder. I turned around. I walked forward. I walked towards my father's white gates. I saw something. I saw something happening. I saw something strange. I saw something strange happening. I saw my white gates. I saw my white gates opening. I saw my gates opening faster. I saw the gates opening faster than a rollercoaster. I walked through the white gates. I was outside the white gates. I was outside my father's royal castle. I walked downwards. I was outside my royal castle. I turned around. I walked forward. I looked forward. I saw my father's royal garage. I went inside the garage. I walked forward. I looked around. I saw plenty of white horses. I walked forward. I looked through the horses. I saw a massive horse. I saw a white massive horse. I touched the white horse. I felt romantic. I pulled the white horse. I pulled him forward. I took the white horse outside the garage. I jumped on the white horse. I sat on the white horse. I saw the white horse. I saw him turning around. I saw him walking. I saw him walking forward. I saw him running. I saw him running towards another nation. I saw him running faster. I saw him running faster and faster. I saw him running faster than a warrior. I saw the prince of England. I saw him sitting on a Roman horse. I saw Prince Harry. I saw him sitting on a white horse. I saw myself sitting on a white horse. I saw me wearing my red garments. I saw me holding my red and white protective armours. I saw myself riding on the white horse. I saw myself riding on my Roman horse. I was riding. I was riding forward. I was riding towards another nation. I was riding faster. I was riding faster and faster. I was riding faster than a pilot. I was riding faster. I was riding faster. I was riding faster than a merchant. I was riding faster than a warrior. I was riding faster than a pirate. I was riding faster than a sailor. I was riding faster. I was riding faster without slowing down. I was riding. I was riding faster and faster. I was riding until I approached somewhere. I approached another nation. I approached Finland. I was riding until I approached someone. I approached a medical doctor. I approached the doctor of Finland. I saw him sitting on a black wagon. I saw his two horses pulling the wagon. I saw the doctor. I saw him behind my horse. I saw him giving me something. I saw him giving me something medical. I saw him giving me water, ice water and ice cream. I grabbed the water, ice water and ice cream. He waved me good luck and he rode forward. I saw my white horse. I saw him running. I saw him running forward. I saw him running faster. I saw him running faster and faster. I saw him running past blue rivers. I saw him running past mountains. I saw him running past snowy mountains. I saw him running past cold rivers. I saw him running past ice waters. I turned around. I saw someone. I saw someone chasing. I saw someone chasing us. I saw three blue wolves. I saw three wolves chasing us. I smacked my white horse. I saw my white horse running. I saw my white horse running forward. I saw my white horse running faster. I turned around. I saw the three wild wolves. I saw them running. I saw them chasing us. I saw them chasing faster. I saw them chasing faster. I saw them chasing closer. I saw them running. I saw them running forward. I saw them running faster. I saw them chasing me and my white horse. I saw them chasing closer and closer. I looked forward. I saw the lion of Judah. I saw Leo. I saw him and millions of his lion armies. I saw them running. I saw them running forward. I saw them running towards the three blue wolves. I saw Leo. I saw him running. I saw him running forward. I saw him running towards the wild wolves. I saw him jumping. I saw him jumping on the three blue wolves. I saw the lion of Judah. I saw Leo. I saw him destroying the three wild Wolves. I saw him protecting the prince of England. I saw him protecting Prince Harry. I saw him protecting me. I saw Leo. I saw the king of Judah. I saw him walking forward. I saw him talking to me. I saw him blessing me. I saw him mentioning the Lords' prayer. I saw something. I saw something happening. I saw something strange. I saw something strange happening. I saw the lion of Judah. I saw my former friend. I saw Leo. I saw him disappearing. I saw him vanishing into the air. I looked at my white horse. I saw him running. I saw him continuing our journey. I saw my white royal horse. I saw him running. I saw him running past another royal kingdom. I saw him running past the gates of mount Turku. I saw him running. I saw him running faster. I saw him running faster and faster. I saw him running faster than a bone merchant I saw him running faster than a merchant warrior. I saw him running. I saw him running faster and faster. I saw him over speeding. I saw him running at a higher speed. I saw him running in emotions. I saw him running farther. I saw him running farther and farther. I was riding. I was riding farther. I was riding faster. I was riding farther from Finland. I was riding farther away from Finland. I was riding past icy rivers. I was riding past snowy forest. I was riding past snowy mountains. I was riding farther. I was riding farther and farther. I was riding past blue rivers. I approached someone. I approached an old man. I approached a wizard. I approached the wizard of mount Turku. I approached wizard Turan. I saw him sitting on his blue horse. I saw him riding on his blue horse. I saw him riding forward. I saw him wearing a blue hoodie. I saw him riding no more. I saw him in front of me. I saw him welcoming me. I saw him welcoming me to mount Turku. I saw wizard Turan. I saw him handing me something. I saw him handing me a red stick. I saw him handing me a long red stick. I grabbed the long red stick. I said thanks to wizard Turan. I saw him smiling. I saw him waving goodbye. I saw him riding on his blue horse. I looked at the long red stick. I pointed the red stick. I pointed the red stick forward. I saw my white horse. I saw my white horse running. I saw my white horse. I saw him running forward. I saw him running faster. I saw him running farther. I saw him running farther from wizard Turan. I saw him running farther from mount Turku.

CHAPTER 3

Prince Harry and His Journey From Finland to Troy

I was riding farther. I was riding farther from mount Turku. I was approaching somewhere. I was approaching another nation. I approached another kingdom. I approached a blue nation. I approached Greece. I was riding. I was riding forward. I was riding faster. I was riding faster and faster. I approached someone. I approached a boy orphan. I was riding no more. I jumped off my white horse. I walked forward. I saw someone. I saw a young boy. I walked towards him. He told me something. He told me about himself. He told me he was a boy orphan. He told me he was a boy prisoner. I was listening to his tale. I asked his name. He told me his name is Troy. He told me his mother had died. He told me his father died. He told me they all died during a battle. I was listening to the boy orphan. I was in front of a boy orphan. He was wearing a large blue hoodie. He was holding something. He was holding something strange. He was holding an old cup. He was holding a big blue cup. I saw the boy orphan. I saw Troy. I saw him talking. I saw him talking to me. I saw him talking about me. I saw him talking about my journey. I saw him talking about my successful journey. I saw him blessing me. I saw him praying for me. I turned around. I walked forward. I walked towards my white horse. I jumped on my white horse. I was sitting on my white horse. I saw the boy orphan. I saw the orphan of Troy. I saw Troy. I saw him turning around. I saw him walking forward. I saw him walking towards me. I saw him in front of me. I saw him shaking. I saw him shivering. I saw him crispy cold. I saw him holding something. I saw him holding a blue cup. I saw him handing me something. I saw him handing me the old cup. I saw him looking at the old cup. I saw him looking at his blue cup. I saw him praying. I saw him waving prayers. I collected his old cup. I collected his blue cup. I looked at his old cup. His cup felt crispy cold. I looked inside his blue cup. I saw something. I saw something inside. I saw water inside. I looked at the boy orphan. I looked at the escaped prisoner. I looked at Troy. I looked at him in his blue eyes. Saw him smiling. I saw him telling me something. He told me to drink the water. I drank his ice cold water. I felt very warm. I felt like a warrior. I felt like a soldier. I saw him waving prayers again. I saw him blessing me again. I saw him waving goodbye. I looked at the boy orphan. I said thanks to the boy orphan. I smiled with the boy orphan. I waved goodbye to the boy orphan. I waved goodbye to the boy prisoner. I waved goodbye to Troy. I pointed my red stick forward. I saw my white horse. I saw my white horse running. I saw my white horse running forward. I saw my white horse. I saw him running. I saw him running farther. I saw him running farther from the boy orphan. I was sitting on my white horse. I was riding on my white horse. I was riding farther from the boy orphan. I was riding farther from Troy. I turned around. I saw the boy orphan. I saw him farther away. I saw him waving his hands. I also waved my hands. I turned around. I was riding forward. I was riding faster. I was riding faster and faster. I was riding faster than a warrior. I rode past Trojan mountains. I rode past Trojan rivers. I rode past Trojan rivers. I rode past Trojan forest. I was riding faster. I was riding faster than a warrior. I saw my white horse. I saw him riding faster. I saw him riding faster and faster. I saw him riding faster than a merchant. I saw him riding faster than a pirate. I saw him riding faster than a warrior. I saw my white horse. I saw him riding. I saw him riding the prince of England. I saw him riding Prince Harry. I saw him riding me. I saw him riding faster. I saw him riding farther. I saw my white horse. I saw him riding farther and faster. I saw my Roman horse. I saw him riding past Trojan mountains. I saw my royal horse. I saw him riding past Trojan rivers. I saw my mysterious horse. I saw him riding past Trojan forest. I saw my special horse. I saw him riding past Trojan valleys. I saw my white horse. I saw him riding forward. I saw him riding towards a massive tunnel. I saw my white horse. I saw my running horse. I saw my riding horse. I saw him entering something. I saw him entering something strange. I saw him entering a tunnel. I saw my white horse. I saw him entering a strange tunnel. I saw my white horse. I saw him running. I saw him running inside a tunnel. I saw the prince of England. I saw Prince Harry. I saw myself. I saw myself riding. I rode faster. I rode inside the tunnel. I rode faster. I rode inside the strange tunnel. I rode farther. I rode farther and faster. I rode faster inside the mysterious tunnel. I rode faster like a warrior. I rode faster like a soldier. I rode faster and farther. I escaped the strange tunnel. I escaped the mysterious tunnel. I escaped the tunnel of darkness. I rode outside the tunnel. I rode, I rode faster. I pointed my red stick. I was riding. I was riding faster. I was riding faster and faster. I was riding faster than a warrior. I was riding faster than a soldier. I was riding like the prince of Troy. I was riding farther. I was riding faster. I approached somewhere. I approached a kingdom. I approached a royal castle. I approached a blue royal castle. I approached the gates of Troy. I was riding. I rode past the blue castle. I rode past the blue royal castle. I rode past the gates of Troy. I rode faster. I rode farther. I rode farther from Troy. I rode past mountains. I rode past rivers. I rode past forest. I rode past valleys. I rode inside another tunnel. I rode past mysterious tombs. I rode farther from Greece. I was approaching another Nation.

CHAPTER 4

Prince Harry and His Journey From Troy to Rome

I was approaching another nation. I approached another blue nation. I approached Italy. I rode past Italian mountains. I rode past rivers. I rode past Italian rivers. I rode past Italian forest. I rode faster. I rode faster on my white horse. I rode faster than a warrior. I rode on my white horse. I rode faster and faster. I rode faster than a merchant bone. I rode harder than a merchant bone. I rode faster like a pirate boat. I rode on my white horse. My white horse was running. I saw him running. I saw him running faster. I saw him running faster and faster. I saw him running faster than a merchant horse. I saw him running faster than a pirate horse. I saw my white horse. I saw him riding. I saw him riding faster than a warrior horse. I saw him riding faster and faster. I saw him riding faster than a pirate warrior. I was sitting on my white horse. I was riding. I was riding faster. I was riding faster and faster. I was riding faster like a royal warrior. I was riding faster like a pirate warrior. I was riding faster like a royal soldier. I approached someone. I approached someone on his white horse. I approached a Roman knight. I saw him wearing large blue garments. I saw him holding a large protective armour. I saw him sitting on a white horse. I asked him for his name. He told me he was a war veteran. He told me he was a Roman knight. He told me he was the knight of Rome. He welcomed me to Italy. He welcomed me to Rome. He prayed for me. He saluted me. He gave me something. He gave me an old cup. I looked inside the cup. I saw blue wine. I looked at him in his eyes. He blinked his blue eyes. He knocked his head. He gave me signs to drink the blue wine. I drank the blue wine. I felt strong. I felt bold. I felt energetic. I felt good. I looked at the war veteran. I looked at the Roman knight. I gave him back the blue cup. I thanked him. I shook his hands. I saluted him. I saw him smiling. I saw the knight of Rome. I saw him smacking his horse. I saw him waving goodbye. I saw him riding. I saw him riding on his white horse. I saw him riding forward. I saw him riding faster. I saw him riding faster and faster. I saw him riding farther. I smacked my white horse. I started riding. I started riding forward. I started riding faster. I started riding faster and faster. I started riding faster like a warrior. I was riding. I was riding faster. I was riding like a warrior. I was riding like a soldier. I rode past mountains. I rode past blue rivers. I rode past Roman warriors. I rode past Roman soldiers. I rode past Roman forest. I was riding faster. I was riding faster like a royal warrior. I was speeding. I was speeding like a rollercoaster. I was riding forward. I approached somewhere. I approached a blue castle. I approached a royal castle. I approached the gates of Rome. I was riding. I was riding on my white horse. I rode past the blue castle. I rode past the blue royal castle. I rode past the gates of Rome. I was riding. I was riding faster. I was riding faster and faster. I rode faster. I rode faster like a royal horse. I rode faster, faster and faster. I was approaching someone. I approached someone. I approached another old man. I approached a war veteran. I approached another war veteran. I saw him sitting on a large black dragon. I saw him wearing a large blue hoodie. I saw his blue eyes. I saw his black dragon. I saw something. I saw something happening. I saw his large dragon. I saw his dragon opening his mighty mouth. I saw his dragon blowing fire. I saw his dragon blowing blue fire. I saw nothing. I saw nothing happening. I saw nothing happening to me. I saw something. I saw something strange. I saw something strange happening. I saw his large black dragon. I saw his dragon speaking. I saw his dragon speaking for protection. I saw his dragon speaking about protecting me. I saw his dragon speaking about protecting me and my white horse. I saw his dragon speaking about my journey. I saw his dragon. I saw his dragon blessing me. I saw his dragon praying. I saw his dragon praying for me. I saw his dragon praying for my journey. I saw the war veteran. I saw the old man. I saw the Roman war veteran. I saw him praying. I saw him praying for me. I saw him praying for my journey. I saw him blessing me. I saw his large dragon. I saw his dragon flapping its wings. I saw his dragon rising upwards. I saw the Roman war veteran. I saw him and his dragon. I saw them upwards. I saw them flying. I saw them flying above the blue sky. I saw them following me. I saw them following me and my white horse. I smacked my white horse. I started riding. I started riding forward. I was riding. I was riding forward. I looked upwards. I looked above the blue sky. I saw the war veteran. I saw him sitting on his dragon. I saw him riding. I saw him riding on his dragon. I saw the Roman war veteran. I saw his large dragon. I saw them flying. I saw them flying upwards. I saw them flying above the blue sky. I saw them flying forward. I saw them following. I saw them following me. I saw them following me and my white horse. I saw them protecting me. I saw them protecting me and my white horse. I saw them flying like a warrior. I saw them flying like a protector. I saw them following me. I saw them following me and my white horse. I was sitting on my royal horse. I was sitting on my white horse. I was riding. I was riding on my white horse. I was riding faster. I was riding faster than a warrior. I was riding like a warrior. I was riding like a prince. I rode past blue rivers. I rode past mountains. I rode past Roman warriors. I rode past Roman soldiers. I rode past Roman knights. I rode past veterans. I rode past orphans. I rode past Roman forest. I rode faster. I rode faster and faster. I looked upwards. I saw the war veteran. I saw him sitting on his large dragon. I saw him riding on his dragon. I saw them riding. I saw them flying. I saw them flying above the blue sky. I saw them flying above the heavenly sky. I saw them protecting me. I saw them protecting me and my royal horse. I saw them protecting me and my white horse. I saw them following me. I saw them following me and my white horse. I was riding. I was riding on my royal horse. I was riding on my white horse. I rode faster. I rode faster and faster. I rode past old buildings. I rode past blue buildings. I rode past snowing buildings. I rode past snowy mountains. I rode faster. I rode faster and faster. I rode faster like a royal warrior. I rode faster and faster. I rode like a soldier. I looked upwards. I saw the Roman veteran. I saw the war veteran. I saw him riding on his dragon. I saw him and his mighty dragon. I saw them flying. I saw them flying forward. I saw them flying above the blue sky. I saw them following me. I saw them following me and my royal horse. I saw them following me and my white horse. I saw them protecting me. I saw them protecting me and my royal horse. I saw them protecting me and my white horse. I was riding. I was riding faster. I rode faster. I rode faster and faster. I rode like a warrior. I rode like a royal prince. I rode like a soldier. I rode like a royal warrior. I rode like a royal soldier. I rode like a merchant. I rode faster. I rode faster and faster. I rode faster than a warrior. I rode faster than a soldier. I was approaching somewhere. I was approaching another nation. I approached somewhere. I approached another nation.

CHAPTER 5

Prince Harry and His Journey From Rome to Netherlands

I approached another nation. I approached a beautiful nation. I approached an orange nation. I approached another beautiful nation. I was riding. I was riding faster. I rode faster. I rode faster than a warrior. I saw beautiful mountains. I saw heavenly mountains. I saw mysterious mountains. I saw beautiful rivers. I saw the heavenly cloud. I saw the heavenly sky. I saw warriors. I saw Netherlands warriors. I saw soldiers. I saw Netherlands soldiers. I saw knights. I saw Netherlands knights. I looked upwards. I saw the protector. I saw the dragon. I saw the war veteran. I saw them flying. I saw them flying above the Netherlands sky. I saw them following. I saw them following me and my white horse. I was riding forward. I was riding faster. I was riding faster and faster. I was riding faster than a merchant rider. I rode faster than a soldier. I rode faster and faster. I was riding like a warrior. I rode like a pirate rider. I rode faster, faster and faster. I was approaching somewhere. I approached another snowy forest. I rode faster. I rode fast inside the snowy forest. I approached someone. I approached a white woman. I saw her wearing an orange hoodie. I saw her with orange eyes. I saw her sitting in a wagon. I saw two white horses. I saw them pulling her wagon. I saw my white horse. I saw my horse running no more. I saw him standing. I saw him in front of the white woman. I saw the white woman. I saw her two horses. I saw her horses pulling her wagon. I saw her horses. I saw them pulling her wagon. I saw the two horses. I saw the white woman. I saw them behind me and my white horse. I saw the white woman. I saw her welcoming me. I saw her welcoming me to the Netherlands. I asked for her name. She told me her name was Naomi. She told me she was a witch doctor. I saw her reaching with her hands. I saw her removing something. I saw her pulling out something. I saw her pulling out an orange cup. I saw her looking inside the cup. I saw her rolling her orange eyes. I saw her orange cup. I saw her handing me the orange cup. I grabbed her orange cup. I looked inside her orange cup. I saw orange water inside the cup. I looked at the witch doctor. I saw her knocking her head. I saw her giving me signs. I saw her giving me signs to drink the orange water. I drank the orange water. I felt cold no more. I felt like a warrior. I felt like a soldier. I felt like a merchant warrior. I felt like a pirate warrior. I felt like a royal warrior. I felt stronger. I felt stronger like a royal soldier. I looked into the eyes of the witch doctor. I thanked her. I saw her smiling. I saw her appreciating my thanks. I saw her smiling like a hero. I reached for my hands. I shook the hands of the witch doctor. I saw her blessing me. I saw her praying for me. I saw her praying for my journey. I saw her waving her horse's strings. I saw the witch doctor. I saw her waving goodbye. I saw her waving me goodbye. I saw her riding in her orange wagon. I saw her waving me and my white horse goodbye. I looked upwards. I saw the war veteran. I saw the dragon. I saw them above the orange sky. I smacked my white horse. I saw my horse running. I saw my horse running faster. I saw my horse running faster and faster. I saw my white horse. I saw my horse riding faster and faster. I saw my horse running. I saw my horse running faster. I saw my horse running faster and faster. I saw my white horse. I saw my horse riding past orange rivers. I saw my horse riding past orange mountains. I saw my white horse riding past orange forest. I looked upwards, I saw the war veteran. I saw the mighty dragon. I saw them flying. I saw them flying above the mountains. I saw them following me. I saw them protecting me. I looked forward. I saw someone. I saw someone approaching me. I saw the lion of Judah. I saw the king of Judah. I saw Leo. I saw him approaching me. I saw my white horse running no more. I saw my white horse. I was in front of the lion of Judah. I saw the lion of Judah. I saw the king of Jerusalem. I saw Leo. I saw him in front of me. I saw him welcoming me. I saw him thanking me. I saw him respecting me. I saw him saluting me. I saw him giving me strong advice. I saw him giving me protection. I saw him believing in me. I saw him having faith in me. I saw him showing me the way forward. I saw him mentioning the Lord's Prayer. I saw him praying for me. I saw the lion of Judah. I saw the king of Jerusalem. I saw something. I saw something. I saw something strange. I saw something strange happening. I saw the lion of Judah. I saw the king of Jerusalem. I saw my protector. I saw his disappearance. I saw him vanishing. I saw him disappearing. I saw him no more. I looked upwards. I saw my heavenly protectors. I saw the war veteran. I saw the mighty dragon. I saw them above the orange mountains. I smacked my white horse. I saw my horse running. I saw my horse running forward. I saw my horse running faster. I saw my horse running faster and faster. I was riding on my white horse. I rode faster. I rode faster and faster. I rode past orange mountains. I rode past orange rivers. I rode past orange forest. I rode past snowy mountains. I rode past icy mountains. I rode past orange warriors. I rode past orange soldiers. I saw warriors. I saw soldiers. I saw veterans. I saw old men. I saw old women. I saw people wearing orange hoodies. I saw women wearing orange hoodies. I saw men wearing orange hoodies. I saw warriors wearing orange hoodies. I saw soldiers wearing orange hoodies. I was riding on my white horse. I rode faster. I rode faster and faster. I rode faster like a warrior. I rode faster like a soldier. I rode faster like a pirate rider. I rode faster than a warrior. I rode faster than a soldier. I rode faster than a pirate. I rode faster than a merchant. I rode faster. I rode faster and faster. I approached somewhere. I approached another forest. I approached another snowing forest. I approached a snowing forest. I entered the snowing forest. I rode faster. I rode faster and faster. I saw my white horse. I saw my horse running no more. I looked upwards. I saw my heavenly protectors. I saw the war veteran. I saw the mighty dragon. I saw them above the orange sky. I saw them flying no more. I saw them following me no more. I approached someone. I approached another old man. I saw him wearing an orange hoodie. I saw him wearing an orange hat. I saw him sitting on an orange horse. I saw him in front of me. I saw him doing something. I saw him smacking his horse. I saw his orange horse. I saw his horse walking. I saw him and his horse behind me. I asked for his name. He told me his name was Nathan. He told me he was a cowboy. I saw him welcoming me. I saw him saluting me. I saw him reaching for something. I saw him giving me an orange cup. I reached my hands for the cup. I grabbed the orange cup. I looked inside the cup. I saw an orange juice. I looked at the cowboy. I looked at him in his orange eyes. I saw him blinking his eyes. I saw him knocking his head. I saw him giving me signs. I saw him giving me signs for drinking the orange juice. I drank the orange juice. I felt heavy. I felt stronger. I felt magnetic. I felt good. I felt cold no more. I felt like a warrior. I felt like a soldier. I felt like a master. I reached my hands forward. I gave his cup back to him. I gave him thanks. I saw Nathan. I saw the old man. I saw the cowboy. I saw him giving me a handshake. I saw him giving me blessings. I saw him giving me words of protection. I saw him waving me goodbye. I saw him smacking his horse. I saw Nathan. I saw the old man. I saw the cowboy and his horse. I saw them riding. I saw them riding forward. I saw them riding faster. I saw them riding faster and faster. I saw them disappearing. I saw Nathan. I saw the cowboy. I saw the old man. I saw his horse. I saw them disappearing. I saw them no more. I looked upwards. I saw the war veteran. I saw the mighty dragon. I saw them flying. I saw them flying above the orange sky. I smacked my white horse. I saw my white horse. I saw my horse running. I saw my horse running faster. I saw my horse running faster and faster. I looked upwards. I saw the war veteran. I saw the mighty dragon. I saw my heavenly protectors. I saw them following me. I saw them protecting me. I smacked my white horse. I smacked my white horse again. I smacked my white horse for the last time. I saw my white horse. I saw my white horse speeding. I saw my white horse running. I saw my white horse running faster. I saw my white horse running faster and faster. I was riding. I was riding on my white horse. I rode faster. I rode faster and faster. I rode faster than a warrior. I rode faster than a soldier. I rode faster, faster and faster. I rode faster than a pirate boat. I saw an orange castle. I rode faster. I rode past the orange castle. I saw a mysterious tunnel. I rode faster. I rode faster inside the mysterious tunnel. I rode faster. I rode faster inside the tunnel of darkness. I rode faster and faster. I rode faster outside the mysterious tunnel. I saw my white horse. I saw my horse running inside the tunnel. I saw my horse running faster outside the tunnel. I rode faster. I rode faster outside the mysterious tunnel. I approached somewhere. I approached a mysterious tomb. I approached an orange tomb. I rode faster. I rode faster and faster. I rode past the mysterious tomb. I rode past the tomb of darkness. I rode past the orange tomb. I approached somewhere. I approached another snowing forest. I rode inside the forest. I rode faster. I rode faster and faster. I came across someone. I came across someone special. I came across Leo. I came across the lion of Judah. I came across the king of Judah. I saw my white horse. I saw him running no more. I saw him in front of Leo. I saw him in front of the lion of Judah. I saw him in front of the king of Judah. I saw him in front of Leo. I saw Leo. I saw the golden lion. I saw the lion of Judah. I saw the king of Jerusalem. I saw him welcoming me. I saw him respecting me. I saw him blessing me. I saw him thanking me. I saw him praying for me. I saw him mentioning the Lord's Prayer. I saw him protecting me. I saw something. I saw something strange. I saw something strange happening. I saw Leo. I saw the lion of Judah. I saw the king of Jerusalem. I saw the king of Judah. I saw him vanishing. I saw him disappearing. I saw his appearance no more. I smacked my white horse. I saw my white horse running. I saw my horse running faster. I looked upwards. I saw my heavenly protectors. I saw the war veteran. I saw the mighty dragon. I saw them protecting. I saw them protecting me. I saw them protecting me and my white horse. I saw them following. I saw them following me. I saw them following me and my white horse. I saw them following my royal horse and me. I smacked my white horse. I saw something. I saw something happening. I saw something strange. I saw something strange happening. I saw me royal horse. I saw my white horse. I saw him over speeding. I saw him running faster. I saw him running faster and faster. I saw him running past snowing forest. I saw him running past orange mountains. I saw him running past orange castles. I rode faster. I approached somewhere. I approached another nation.

CHAPTER 6

Prince Harry and His Journey From The Netherlands to Romania

I approached another Roman nation. I approached Romania. I entered Romania. I rode inside snowing forest. I rode forward. I rode past snowing woodlands. I was riding. I was riding faster. I was riding faster and faster. I was riding faster than a merchant warrior. I rode faster. I rode faster and faster. I rode faster like a merchant soldier. I rode through snowing woodlands. I rode forward. I rode faster. I rode faster and faster. I approached someone. I approached an old woman. I saw her wearing a golden hoodie. I saw her sitting inside a gold wagon. I saw her two gold horses. I saw her horses pulling the wagon. I saw her horses pulling her wagon no more. I saw my white royal horse. I saw my horse riding no more. I saw the white woman. I saw her in front of me and my white horse. I looked upwards. I saw my heavenly protectors. I saw the war veteran and the dragon. I saw them flying no more. I looked forward. I saw the white woman. I saw her speaking. I saw her welcoming me. I asked for her name. She told me she was called Ruth Rodina. She told me she was a woman reverend. She told me she was the reverend of Romania. I saw her doing something. I saw her reaching for her hands. I saw her removing something. I saw her removing a round bowl. I saw her removing a golden bowl. I saw her holding the golden bowl. I saw her doing something. I saw her doing something strange. I saw her looking inside the bowl. I saw her rolling her golden eyes. I saw her doing something. I saw her praying. I saw her waving prayers. I saw her praying over the bowl. I saw her reaching for her hand. I saw her giving me the golden bowl. I looked at the white reverend. I looked at the reverend of Romania. I reached for my hands. I grabbed the golden bowl. I looked inside the bowl. I saw golden water. I saw gold water inside the bowl. I looked into her golden eyes. I saw her doing something. I saw her blinking her eyes. I saw her knocking her head. I saw her giving me orders. I saw her giving me signs. I saw her ordering me to drink the golden water. I looked into her golden eyes. I drank the golden water. I felt stronger. I felt like a warrior. I felt very energetic. I felt warmed. I felt like a soldier. I felt glorious. I felt victorious. I looked into her golden eyes. I reached for my hands. I gave her golden bowl. I gave her golden bowl back to her. I saw her speaking. She told me to remain strong. She told me not to fear. She told me not to be afraid of anything. She told me not to fear anyone. She told me the Lord is with me. She prayed for me. She blessed me. I saw her waving her horses' strings. I saw the woman reverend. I saw the white reverend. I saw her wearing a large gold hoodie. I saw her smiling. I saw her smiling with me. I saw her waving me goodbye. I saw her horses. I saw them running. I saw the white reverend. I saw the woman reverend. I saw the reverend of Romania. I saw her sitting in a golden wagon. I saw her riding in a golden wagon. I saw her golden horses. I saw her horses pulling her wagon. I saw her horses running. I saw her riding in her wagon. I saw her waving me goodbye. I saw her riding. I saw her riding behind me. I saw her riding past me. I smacked my white horse. I smacked my royal horse. I smacked my warrior horse. I saw my white horse. I saw my white horse running. I looked upwards. I saw my two protectors. I saw the war veteran. I saw the heavenly dragon. I saw them flying. I saw them flying above the golden sky. I saw them flying forward. I saw the war veteran. I saw my heavenly protector. I saw him riding. I saw him riding on the dragon. I saw him flying. I saw him flying on the dragon. I saw him following me and my royal horse. I saw my heavenly protector. I saw the heavenly dragon. I saw him flying. I saw him flying above the golden sky. I saw my heavenly protector. I saw the heavenly dragon. I saw him protecting. I saw him protecting me and my white horse. I saw the war veteran. I saw the heavenly dragon. I saw them flying. I saw them flying faster. I saw them flying faster than a heavenly warrior. I saw them riding. I saw them riding faster. I saw them riding faster than a heavenly warrior. I smacked my white horse. I smacked him harder. I saw my royal horse. I saw him running. I saw him running faster. I smacked him harder. I smacked him harder and harder. I saw my white horse. I saw my royal horse. I saw him running. I saw him running faster. I saw him running faster and faster. I saw my running horse. I saw him approaching a mysterious tomb. I saw him entering the mysterious tomb. I saw him running inside the mysterious tomb. I saw my running horse. I saw him inside the mysterious tomb. I was sitting on my white horse. I was riding on my royal horse. I looked inside the tomb. I saw no one. I saw darkness. I suddenly saw light. I looked around me. I saw plenty golden lions. I looked forward. I saw someone. I saw someone walking forward. I saw someone walking towards me and my horse. I saw someone in front of me and my white horse. I saw a former friend. I saw Leo. I saw the lion of Judah. I saw the king of Jerusalem. I saw the lion king. I saw him speaking. I saw him blessing me. I saw him saluting me. I saw him congratulating me. I saw him welcoming me. I saw him respecting me. I saw the lion of Judah. I saw him praying for me. I saw him mentioning the Lord's Prayer. I saw the lion of Judah. I saw him walking. I saw him walking forward. I saw him walking towards the mysterious gates. I saw him in front of the mysterious gates. I saw him doing something. I saw him doing something strange. I saw him roaring. I saw him roaring harder. I saw him roaring harder and harder. I saw something. I saw something strange happening. I saw the mysterious gates. I saw the mysterious gates opening. I saw the gates opening faster. I saw the lion of Judah. I saw him ordering me and my white horse. I saw him ordering me outside the tomb. I smacked my white horse. I smacked my royal horse. I saw him running. I saw him running slowly. I saw him outside the mysterious tomb. I looked forward. I saw someone. I saw someone. Walking. I saw someone walking behind me. I saw the lion of Judah. I saw Leo. I saw him behind me. I saw him waving me prayers. I saw him blessing me. I saw him mentioning the Lord's Prayer again. I felt stronger. I felt like a warrior. I felt like a royal soldier. I felt like a royal warrior. I felt magnetic. I felt energetic. I felt magnificent. I saw the lion of Judah. I saw the lion king. I saw something. I saw something strange. I saw something happening. I saw something strange happening. I looked behind me. I saw the Lion King. I saw the lion of Judah. I saw him vanishing. I saw him disappearing. I smacked my white horse. I saw him running. I smacked my royal horse. I saw him running faster. I smacked him again. I saw my white horse. I saw my royal horse. I saw him running. I saw him running faster. I saw him running faster and faster. I saw him over speeding. I was riding on my white horse. I rode on my royal horse. I rode faster. I rode faster and faster. I rode faster like a warrior. I rode faster like a royal warrior. I rode faster like a royal soldier. I rode faster than a royal warrior. I rode faster than a royal soldier. I rode inside snowing forest. I rode past snowing woodlands. I rode past muddy woodlands. I rode past snowing mountains. I rode past raining forest. I rode past raining woodlands. I looked upwards. I saw my heavenly protectors. I saw the war veteran. I saw the heavenly dragon. I saw them flying. I saw them flying forward. I saw them protecting. I saw them protecting me and my royal horse. I saw them following. I saw them following me and my royal horse. I saw them flying. I saw them flying above the Romanian sky. I saw the war veteran. I saw him sitting on the heavenly dragon. I saw him riding on his heavenly dragon. I saw him riding like a warrior. I saw him riding like a soldier. I saw him following me and my royal horse. I saw him and his heavenly dragon. I saw my heavenly protectors. I saw them protecting me. I saw the war veteran and his heavenly dragon. I saw them following me and my white horse. I looked forward. I smacked my white horse. I smacked him harder. I smacked him harder again. I saw my white horse. I saw him running. I saw him running faster. I saw him running faster and faster. I saw him over speeding. I saw him running faster than a warrior. I saw him running faster than a soldier. I saw him approaching somewhere. I approached somewhere. I approached a raining forest. I rode inside the raining forest. I rode past raining woodlands. I saw my white horse. I saw him stepping on muddy woodlands. I rode past raining woodlands. I approached someone. I approached another woman. I saw her wearing a large gold hoodie. I saw her sitting on a golden horse. I asked for her name. I saw her replying me. She told me she was called Hana Rohan. She told me she was a witch doctor. I saw her welcoming me. I saw her reaching out her hand for something. I saw her pulling out something. I saw her pulling out a long red magic stick. I saw her holding a long red magic stick. I saw her rolling her golden eyes. I looked inside her rolling eyes. I saw her eyes rolling. I saw something. I saw something strange. I saw something strange happening. I saw her eyes turning into red. I saw her saying something. I saw her charming the long red stick. I saw her saying something on the red stick. I saw her speaking a language. I saw her speaking another language. I never understood her language. I saw the witch doctor. I saw her handing me the long red stick. I looked into her eyes. I reached for my hands. I grabbed the red stick. I felt stronger. Felt warmer. I felt like a warrior. I felt like a soldier. I felt magnetic. I felt energetic. I felt energetic. I felt heavier. I felt like a royal warrior. I felt like a royal soldier. I looked forward. I saw the witch doctor. I looked inside her red eyes. I saw her doing something. I saw her spinning her eyes. I saw her smiling. I saw her saluting me. I saw her welcoming me. I saw her respecting me. I saw her waving me goodbye. I saw her smacking her golden horse. I saw her golden horse. I saw her horse running. I saw the witch doctor. I saw her riding on her golden horse. I saw her riding faster. I saw her riding fast behind me. I turned around. I saw the Roman witch. I saw the witch doctor. I saw her riding on her golden horse. I turned around. I smacked my white horse. I saw my horse running. I was sitting on my royal horse. I was riding on my royal horse. I rode past raining woodlands. I rode past snowing woodlands. I rode faster. I rode faster and faster. I rode past raining mountains. I rode past snowing mountains. I rode faster. I rode faster and faster. I looked upwards. I saw my protectors. I saw the war veteran. I saw the heavenly dragon. I saw them flying. I saw them flying above snowing mountains. I saw them flying above raining mountains. I saw the war veteran. I saw him sitting on his heavenly dragon. I saw him flying. I saw him flying forward. I saw him riding. I saw him riding forward. I saw him riding faster. I saw him protecting. I saw him protecting me and my white horse. I saw him following. I saw him following me and my royal horse. I saw his heavenly dragon. I saw the dragon flying. I saw the dragon flying forward. I saw the dragon flying above raining mountains. I saw his dragon flying above snowing mountains. I saw his dragon flying faster. I saw his dragon protecting me. I saw his heavenly dragon following me and my running horse. I looked forward. I saw my white horse. I saw my royal horse. I saw my riding horse. I saw my horse riding. I saw my horse riding faster. I saw my horse riding faster than a warrior. I saw my horse riding faster than a soldier. I saw my strong horse. I saw my magnificent horse. I saw my white horse. I saw my royal horse. I saw my horse running faster and faster. I saw my horse approaching another nation.

CHAPTER 7

Prince Harry and His Journey From Romania to Germany

I was riding. I was riding on my horse. I approached another nation. I approached Germany. I entered another nation. I entered Germany. I was riding. I was riding faster. I rode through snowing forest. I entered snowing woodlands. I was riding. I was riding faster. I was riding faster and faster. I looked upwards. I saw the war veteran. I saw the dragon. I saw my heavenly protectors. I saw them upwards. I saw them flying no more. I saw my white horse. I saw my royal horse. I saw my horse not running. I saw my horse running no more. I looked forward. I saw someone. I saw someone coming. I saw a white woman. I saw an old woman. I saw her wearing a black hoodie. I saw her having strange nails. I saw her strange long nails. I saw her ducking. I saw her ducking forward. I saw her ducking towards me. I saw her in front of me. I asked for her name. She told me she was called Sophia. She told me she was an old witch. She welcomed me to Germany. She removed a cup from her pockets. She turned around. I saw her walking forward. I saw her walking towards a river. I saw her ducking. I saw her in front of the river. I saw her fetching water. I saw her carrying the watery cup. I saw her in front of me. I saw her telling me something. I saw her telling me to open my mouth. I opened my mouth. I saw her pouring warm water. She poured warm water inside my mouth. I drank her warm water. I drank the warm water inside her cup. I felt stronger. I felt magnetic. I felt magnificent. I felt warmer. I felt mysterious. I felt like a soldier. I felt like a warrior. I smiled with her. I thanked her. I looked at her inside her eyes. I saw something. I saw something strange. I saw her white eyes. I saw her white eyes rolling. I saw her white eyes turning black. I saw her telling me something. I saw her talking about my journey. She told me not to fear. She told me not to give up. She told me to be bold, strong and magnetic. She told me to be happy. She told me to remain intelligent. She told me to remain a royal warrior. She told me to remain a royal soldier. She told me to be fearless. I saw the witch in the woodlands. I met Sophia. I met the witch in Germany. I saw her praying. I saw her praying for me. I saw her praying out heavenly spells. I saw her walking forward. I saw her in front of me. I saw her reaching out her hands. I saw her reaching out her strange nails. I saw her reaching out for her long nails. I saw her grabbing my hands. I saw her shaking my hands. I felt energetic. I felt like a superhero. I felt like a soldier. I felt like a warrior. I felt magnetic. I looked inside her eyes. I saw her waving goodbye. I saw her waving me goodbye. I smiled with her. She smiled with me. I ducked my head downwards. I saluted Sophia. I saluted the witch. I saluted the witch of the snowing woodlands. I smacked my white horse. I saw my horse running. I saw my white horse. I saw my royal horse riding. I saw my horse riding forward. I saw my horse running. I saw my horse running faster. I saw my horse running faster and faster. I saw my horse running faster than a superhero. I was sitting on my white horse. I was riding on my royal horse. I was riding faster. I was riding faster and faster. I was riding faster than a merchant soldier. I looked upwards. I saw my two heavenly protectors. I saw the war veteran. I saw the heavenly dragon. I saw them flying upwards. I saw them flying forward. I saw them protecting me. I saw them protecting me and my royal horse. I saw them flying faster. I saw them flying faster and faster. I saw them flying faster like a warrior. I saw them flying faster like a soldier. I saw them flying above snowing woodlands. I saw them flying above snowing forest. I saw them flying above snowing mountains. I was sitting on my white horse. I was riding on my royal horse. I rode faster. I rode faster and faster. I rode inside snowing woodlands. I rode past snowing forest. I rode past snowing mountains. I rode past snowing rivers. I rode past snowing castles. I approached another tunnel. I approached another snowing tunnel. I approached a tunnel of darkness. I rode inside the tunnel of darkness. I rode faster. I rode faster and faster. I rode faster than darkness. I rode faster than a warrior. I rode faster like a warrior. I rode faster like a royal warrior. I rode inside the tunnel of darkness. I saw everywhere in darkness. I smacked my white horse. I smacked my royal horse. I saw something. I saw something happening. I saw something strange. I saw something strange happening. I saw my white horse. I saw my royal horse. I saw my running horse. I saw my horse over speeding. I saw my horse running. I saw my horse running faster, faster and faster. I saw my horse over speeding like a warrior horse. I saw my royal horse over speeding like a royal horse. I was riding on my white horse. I was riding inside a tunnel of darkness. I was riding like a dangerous warrior. I smacked my royal horse. I smacked my white horse. I smacked my warrior horse for the third time. I saw something. I saw something happening. I saw my horse over speeding. I saw my horse riding faster. I saw my horse running faster. I saw my horse running like a royal warrior. I saw my horse approaching somewhere. I saw my horse outside the tunnel of darkness. I saw my horse running. I saw my horse running faster. I saw my horse running faster and faster. I saw my horse approaching somewhere. I was riding on my horse. I rode faster. I rode faster and faster. I rode outside the tunnel of darkness. I approached somewhere. I approached another snowing forest. I rode inside the snowing forest. I rode faster. I rode faster and faster. I approached another snowing woodlands. I rode inside the snowing woodlands. I approached someone. I approached a young girl. I saw her wearing a white hoodie. I saw her sitting closer to a small lake. I saw five ducks floating in the lake. I saw the young girl. I saw her holding two loaves of bread. I saw her doing something. I saw her feeding the five ducks. I saw my horse running no more. I looked upwards. I saw my heavenly protectors. I saw the war veteran. I saw the heavenly dragon. I saw them flying no more. I looked forward. I saw the young girl. I saw her turning around. I saw her facing forward. I saw her looking at me. I saw her walking forward. I saw her walking towards me. I saw her in front of me. I saw the young girl. I saw her welcoming me. I saw her looking upwards. I saw her looking at the war veteran. I saw her looking at the mighty dragon. I saw her welcoming them. I looked at her inside her blue eyes. I asked for her name. She told me she was called Lucy. She told me she was a girl orphan. I saw her putting her hands inside her pocket. I saw her removing something. I saw her removing a black cup. I saw her giving me the black cup. I grabbed the black cup. I looked inside the black cup. I saw boiling hot water. I looked at her inside her eyes. I saw her doing something. I saw her blinking her blue eyes. I saw her bowing her head downwards. I saw her giving me signals. I saw her giving me signs for me to drink the boiling hot water. I drank the boiling hot water. I felt magnificent. I felt magnetic. I felt heavenly. I felt stronger. I felt like a warrior. I felt like a royal warrior. I felt like a royal soldier. I felt fearless. I felt heavenly. I looked at Lucy. I looked at the girl orphan. I saw her smiling. I saw her saluting me. I saw her respecting me. I saw her obeying me. I saw her praying for me. I looked inside her blue eyes. I looked at the girl orphan. I thanked her. I shook her hands. I saw her praying for me and my heavenly protectors. I saw her waving me goodbye. I waved goodbye to Lucy. I waved the girl orphan goodbye. I smacked my horse. I smacked my white horse. I smacked my royal horse. I saw my horse running. I saw my horse running faster. I saw my horse running faster and faster. I was sitting on my horse. I was riding on my horse. I rode faster. I rode faster and faster. I rode past snowing woodlands. I rode past snowing mountains. I rode past snowing rivers. I looked upwards. I saw my two heavenly protectors. I saw them flying. I saw them flying faster. I saw them protecting me. I saw them following me. I smacked my white horse. I saw my horse running faster. I saw my horse running faster and faster. I saw my horse approaching somewhere.

CHAPTER 8

Prince Harry and His Journey From Germany to Normandy

I saw my white horse approaching another nation. I saw my royal horse approaching Normandy. I was riding on my royal horse. I rode faster. I rode faster and faster. I entered another nation. I entered Normandy. I entered France. I rode faster. I rode faster and faster. I rode past dead bodies. I rode past the battle of Normandy. I rode past snowing rivers. I rode past snowing mountains. I rode faster. I rode faster and faster. I rode faster than a warrior. I rode faster than Norman warriors. I rode faster than Norman soldiers. I smacked my white horse. I smacked my royal horse. I saw my white horse. I saw my royal horse. I saw my horse running. I saw my royal horse running. I saw my white horse running. I saw my horse running faster. I saw my horse running faster than a Norman horse. I was riding on my royal horse. I rode faster. I rode faster and faster. I approached somewhere. I approached another snowing forest. I rode inside the snowing forest. I smacked my royal horse. I smacked my white horse. I saw my horse running. I saw my horse running faster. I saw my horse running faster and faster. I was riding on my royal horse. I rode faster. I rode faster and faster. I rode faster than a Norman soldier. I rode inside snowing forest. I rode past snowing woodlands. I approached someone. I approached my best friend. I approached the lion of Judah. I approached the king of Jerusalem. I approached my heavenly protector. I approached Leo. I saw my white horse. I saw him running no more. I looked upwards. I saw the war veteran. I saw the heavenly dragon. I saw my heavenly protectors. I saw them flying no more. I saw them protecting no more. I looked forward. I saw the lion of Judah. I saw my best friend. I saw the lion king. I saw Leo. I saw my heavenly protector. I saw him walking forward. I saw him walking towards me. I saw him behind me. I saw him speaking. I saw him speaking to me. I saw him welcoming me. I saw him welcoming me to Normandy. I saw him welcoming me to France. I saw him congratulating me. I saw him congratulating me about my mysterious journey. I saw him congratulating me for coming farther. I saw him blessing me. I saw him looking upwards. I saw him thanking the war veteran. I saw him thanking the heavenly dragon. I saw him thanking them for protecting me and my horse. I saw him blessing me and my royal horse. I saw my best friend. I saw the lion king. I saw the lion of Judah. I saw my royal lion. I saw him blessing me and my horse. I saw him mentioning the Lord's Prayer. I saw his thanks. I saw the lion king. I saw the lion of Judah. I saw my heavenly protector. I saw him waving goodbye. I saw him waving me goodbye. I saw him waving the war veteran and the dragon goodbye. I saw him waving my heavenly protectors goodbye. I saw the lion of Judah. I saw the lion king. I saw Leo. I saw something happening. I saw something strange. I saw something strange happening. I saw the lion king. I saw the lion of Judah. I saw him vanishing. I saw him disappearing. I saw his immediate disappearance. I saw his existence no more. I smacked my white horse. I smacked my royal horse. I smacked my white horse. I smacked my royal horse. I saw my white horse. I saw my royal horse. I saw my horse running. I saw my horse running faster. I saw my horse running past snowing woodlands. I saw my white horse running past raining woodlands. I saw my white horse. I saw my running horse. I saw my horse running faster. I saw my horse running faster and faster. I saw my white horse running faster, faster and faster. I was riding on my white horse. I was riding on my royal horse. I rode inside another snowing forest. I rode past snowing woodlands. I rode past raining woodlands. I looked upwards. I saw the war veteran and his dragon. I saw them flying. I saw them flying upwards. I saw them flying faster. I saw them flying faster than a Norman dragon. I saw them flying above snowing woodlands. I saw them flying above raining woodlands. I smacked my white horse. I smacked my royal horse. I saw something. I saw something strange. I saw something strange happening. I saw my white horse. I saw my royal horse. I saw my horse over speeding. I saw my horse running faster. I saw my horse running faster and faster. I saw my horse running faster than Norman horses. I smacked my white horse. I smacked my royal horse. I saw my horse over speeding. I was riding on my royal horse. I was riding on my white horse. I rode faster than Norman soldiers. I approached somewhere. I approached another snowing woodlands. I smacked my white horse. I smacked my royal horse. I saw my white horse. I saw my royal horse. I saw my horse running. I saw my horse running faster. I saw my horse running faster and faster. I saw my horse running faster, faster and faster. I was riding on my mysterious horse. I rode faster. I rode faster and faster. I rode past another snowing woodlands. I approached someone. I approached a white man. I approached a Norman cowboy. I saw my horse running no more. I looked upwards. I saw the war veteran and the dragon. I saw my heavenly protectors. I saw them flying no more. I saw them protecting no more. I saw them detecting no more. I looked forward. I saw someone. I saw an old man. I saw a white man. I saw him sitting on his brown horse. I saw him wearing a blue jacket. I saw his jackets covered in snows. I saw him wearing a round black hat. I saw him looking like a cowboy. I saw him riding on his brown horse. I saw him riding no more. I saw him in front of me and my horse. I saw the old man. I saw the old cowboy. I saw him speaking. I saw him welcoming me. I saw him welcoming me to France. I saw him welcoming me to Normandy. I saw him asking for my name. I told him I was Harry. I told him I was a prince from England. I told him I was the prince of England.

I looked at the white man. I looked at the old cowboy. I saw him smiling. I asked for his name. He told me his name was Peter Norman. I saw him reaching for my hands. I saw him shaking my hands. I saw him smiling. I saw him welcoming me. I saw him welcoming the war veteran and his dragon. I looked at him inside his eyes. I saw his blue eyes. I saw the old cowboy. I saw him reaching out his hands. I saw him putting his hands inside his pocket. I saw him pulling out something. I saw him removing something. I saw him removing a blue cup. I saw him reaching for my hands. I saw him delivering me the cup. I reached my hands forward. I grabbed the cup. I looked inside the cup. I saw blue ice water. I looked at the cowboy. I looked into his eyes. I saw him blinking his eyes. I saw him knocking his head. I saw him giving me signs for drinking the ice water. I looked inside the icy cup. I drank the ice water. I felt magnetic. I felt stronger. I felt like a Norman soldier. I felt like a Norman warrior. I felt like a royal soldier. I felt energetic. I felt magnificent. I felt heavier. I felt like a warrior. I looked at the cowboy. I looked at the Norman cowboy. I gave him thanks. I thanked him. I shook his hands. I saw the old man. I saw the Norman cowboy. I saw the old man. I saw the old white man. I saw him welcoming me again. I saw him welcoming the war veteran and the dragon again. I saw him smiling. I saw him blessing me. I saw him giving me something. I saw him reaching for his hands. I saw him putting his hands inside his pocket. I saw him removing something. I saw him pulling out something. I saw him pulling out a booklet. I saw the booklet. I saw a Red Booklet. I saw the old cowboy. I saw him speaking. He told me about the booklet. He told me about the Book of Freedom. He told me the booklet was the Book of Freedom. He told me the booklet must be given to two presidents. He told me the booklet must be handed to two presidents for signing. He told me the two presidents must sign the Book of Freedom for a peace treaty. He told me the Book of Freedom was the key. He told me the Book of Freedom was for ending the battle.

He told me it was for ending the battle between two warring nations. I saw the old man. I saw the Norman cowboy. I saw Peter Norman. I saw him handing me the booklet. I grabbed the Red Booklet. I observed the booklet. I opened the Red Booklet. I opened the Book of Freedom. I looked inside the Red Booklet. I looked inside the Book of Freedom. I saw something. I saw something strange. I saw something mysterious. I saw something. I saw something dangerous. I saw a strange battle. I saw a mysterious battle. I saw a battle of two armies. I saw a battle between two nations. I saw two bloody armies. I saw two bloody armies fighting. I saw two bloody nations. I saw two bloody nations fighting. I saw two bloody nations battling. I saw two bloody nations at war. I felt emotionless. I felt fearful. I felt saddened. I felt disappointed. I felt worried. I felt disrespectful. I felt like a stranger. I felt like a soldier. I felt something. I felt something happening. I felt energetic. I felt magnetic. I felt magnificent. I felt like a cowboy. I felt like a warrior. I felt like a Norman warrior. I felt like a Norman cowboy. I looked at the old man. I looked at the Norman cowboy. I saw him speaking. He told me about the two warring nations. He told me to hurry. He told me to ride faster. He told me to arrive faster. He told me to arrive before the end of the battle. He told me to hurry and ride faster. He told me to continue my mysterious journey. He told me to continue my journey without fear. He told me to be fearless. He told me to continue my journey with compassion. He reached for my hands. He gave me a handshake. I gave him a thanks. I saw the old man. I saw the Norman cowboy. I saw him doing something. I saw him blessing me. I saw him welcoming me again. I saw him looking upwards. I saw him looking at the war veteran and the dragon. I saw him looking at my heavenly protectors. I saw him blessing them. I saw him welcoming them. I saw the war veteran and the dragon. I saw them giving him thanks. I saw them respecting the Norman cowboy. I saw them respecting Peter Norman. I saw the Norman cowboy. I saw him waving goodbye. I saw him waving me goodbye. I saw him waving the veteran and his dragon goodbye. I saw the Norman cowboy. I saw him waving everyone goodbye. I saw the Norman cowboy. I saw him smacking his brown horse. I saw him smacking his horse again. I saw his horse running. I saw his horse running faster. I saw the Norman cowboy. I saw him sitting on his brown horse. I saw him riding. I saw him riding forward. I saw him riding faster. I saw him riding past me and my horse. I was sitting on royal horse. I turned around. I saw Peter Norman. I saw the Norman cowboy. I saw him riding. I saw him riding on his brown horse. I saw him riding inside snowing forest. I saw him riding past snowing woodlands. I saw him riding faster. I saw him riding farther. I turned around. I looked at the Red Booklet. I looked at the Book of Freedom. I opened my pocket. I placed the Red Booklet inside my pocket. I dropped the Book of Freedom inside my pocket. I closed my pocket. I looked forward. I smacked my white horse. I smacked my royal horse. I saw my horse running. I saw my horse running faster. I saw my horse running faster and faster. I was sitting on my white horse. I was riding on my royal horse. I was riding faster. I was riding faster and faster. I looked upwards. I saw the war veteran and the dragon. I saw my heavenly protectors. I saw them flying. I saw them flying above snowing mountains. I saw the war veteran. I saw him riding on his dragon. I saw him riding faster. I smacked my white horse. I smacked my royal horse. I saw my royal horse running. I saw my royal horse running faster. I saw my white horse running faster and faster. I was sitting on my royal horse. I was riding faster. I rode faster. I rode faster and faster. I rode past snowing woodlands. I rode past Norman Rivers. I rode past Norman soldiers. I rode past dead soldiers. I rode past Norman mountains. I rode past Norman castles. I rode past Norman warriors. I rode inside Norman tunnels. I rode farther. I rode farther and farther. I was approaching somewhere. I continued riding. I rode, rode and rode. I rode until my horse started speeding. I saw my horse over speeding. I saw my horse approaching somewhere. I saw the war veteran and the dragon approaching somewhere. I was approaching another Nation. I approached another nation.

CHAPTER 9

Prince Harry and His Journey From Normandy to Hungary

I approached another nation. I approached another snowing nation. I approached Hungary. I was riding. I rode faster. I rode faster and faster. I rode faster than a warrior. I rode faster than a soldier. I rode faster, faster and faster. I rode like a royal prince. I rode like a royal warrior. I rode past snowing mountains. I rode past snowing rivers. I rode past raining mountains. I entered another snowing forest. I rode faster. I rode faster and faster. I rode faster than a royal soldier. I rode inside snowing forest. I rode past another snowing woodlands. I approached an old woman. I saw an old woman. I saw a white woman. I saw a white Hungarian woman. I saw her wearing a large red hoodie. I saw her sitting inside a wagon. I saw her sitting inside a red wagon. I saw two red horses. I saw her two red horses. I saw them pulling her wagon. I saw her two red horses. I saw them pulling her wagon no more. I saw them in front of me. I saw my royal horse. I saw my white horse. I saw my horse running no more. I saw my horse in front of the white woman. I looked upwards. I saw the war veteran and his dragon. I saw them flying no more. I saw them detecting no more. I looked forward. I saw the white woman. I saw the Hungarian woman. I looked at her. I saw her looking at me. I saw her welcoming me. I saw her welcoming the war veteran and his dragon. I looked at the old woman. I looked at the white woman. I looked at the Hungarian woman. I saw her looking at me. I asked for her name. She told me she was called Linda Hunburger. She told me she was a witch hunter. She told me she was a witch. She told me she was a huntswoman. I asked her a question. I asked her who she was hunting for. She replied me. She replied me in a softer tone. She replied me in a lower voice. I heard echoes of her crescendos. She replied me she hunted for humans. She told me she hunted for human bodies. I asked her another question. She replied me in a lower tone of voice. I heard her echoes of her witchcraft crescendos. I asked her why she hunted for humans. She replied me she hunted for humans because she was a witch huntswoman. She replied me she hunted for humans because of her witchcraft. I asked her another question. I asked her where she was riding towards. She replied me in a lower tone of voice. I heard another echo of her witchcraft crescendos. She replied me she was seeking for humans. She replied me she was searching for a huntsman. She replied me she was searching for human bloods. She replied me she was searching for human bodies. She replied me she was searching for dead bodies. I saw her reach out her hands. I saw her putting her hands inside her wagon. I saw her removing something. I saw her removing something strange. I saw her removing a red cup. I saw her holding a red cup. I looked inside her red eyes. I saw something. I saw something strange. I saw her rolling her eyes. I saw her spinning her red eyes. I saw her looking at me. I saw her reaching for her hands. I saw her delivering me the red cup. I looked inside her red eyes. She gave me signs for grabbing the cup. I saw her blinking her red eyes. I saw her knocking her head. I looked deeply inside her red eyes. I reached for my hands. I reached my hands forward. I grabbed her red cup. I looked inside her red cup. I saw red bloody water. I looked inside her red eyes. I saw her blinking her red eyes. I saw her bowing her head. I saw her smiling. I saw her giving me signals. I saw her giving me signs for drinking the bloody water. I looked at the old woman. I looked at the witch huntswoman. I looked at the Hungarian old woman. I looked into her Romantic eyes. I saw her smiling. I drank the bloody water. I felt magnetic. I felt heavier. I felt stronger. I felt magnificent. I felt like a royal hero. I felt like a royal warrior. I felt like a royal soldier. I felt like a royal prince. I felt like a huntsman. I felt victorious. I felt glorious. I felt more intelligent. I looked at the white woman. I thanked her. I gave her thanks. I saw her smiling. I saw her smiling again. I smiled with her. She saw me smiling. She welcomed me. I saw her head downwards. I saw her saluting me. I saw her saluting the war veteran and his dragon. I dropped my head downwards. I saluted her. She saw me saluting her. I looked upwards. I saw the war veteran. I saw his head downwards. I saw him saluting the witch huntswoman. I saw him saluting the Hungarian old woman. I saw him saluting the Hungarian witch huntswoman. I saw the Hungarian huntswoman. I saw the witch huntswoman. I saw her head downwards. I saw her saluting me. I saw her saluting the war veteran and his dragon. I saw her head upwards. I saw her waving her two strings. I saw her two red horses. I saw them walking. I saw them walking forward. I saw her two red horses. I saw them behind me and my royal horse. I saw the Hungarian huntswoman. I saw the old woman. I saw the white old woman. I saw the witch huntswoman. I saw her sitting inside her red wagon. I saw her behind me. I saw her reaching her hands forward. I saw her grabbing my hands. I saw her holding my hands. I saw her head downwards. I saw her kissing my hands. I saw her head upwards. I saw her thanking me. She gave me thanks. I saw her smiling. I looked inside her red eyes. I saw her blinking her eyes. I saw her knocking her head. I saw her speaking. I saw her speaking for glory. I saw her praying for me. I saw her mentioning the Lord's Prayer. I saw her blessing me. I saw her speaking about my journey. I saw her performing spells and magic. I saw her performing miracles. I saw the huntswoman. I saw the witch huntswoman. I saw her waving me goodbye. I saw her waving the veteran and his dragon goodbye. I saw her inside her red wagon. I saw her waving her two strings. I saw her two red horses. I saw her horses running. I saw her horses running forward. I saw the Hungarian old woman. I saw the witch huntswoman. I saw her riding. I saw her riding forward. I saw her riding faster. I waved her goodbye. I turned around. I reached for my royal hands. I placed my hands inside my royal pocket. I removed something. I removed something special. I removed something inside my royal pocket. I removed the Red Booklet. I removed the Book of Freedom. I opened the Red Booklet. I opened the Book of Freedom. I looked inside the Book of Freedom. I saw something. I saw something strange. I saw something mysterious. I saw something incredible. I saw two warring nations. I saw two nations in battle. I saw two warring nations. I saw two warring nations fighting. I saw two warring armies. I saw two armies fighting. I saw two bloody armies fighting. I saw two warring armies. I saw two warring armies fighting. I saw plenty of dead soldiers. I saw plenty of dead warriors. I saw plenty of dead armies. I saw plenty of fighting armies. I saw plenty of fighting soldiers. I saw plenty of fighting warriors. I saw plenty of fighting women. I saw plenty of fighting men. I saw plenty of orphanages. I saw plenty of boy orphans. I saw plenty of girl orphans. I saw plenty of poor children. I saw plenty of damaged buildings. I saw plenty of damaged trees. I saw two blood nations at war. I closed the Red Booklet. I closed the Book of Freedom. I felt disappointed. I felt anxious. I felt like a stranger. I felt worried. I felt like a warrior. I felt like a soldier. I felt magnetic. I felt like a royal warrior. I dropped the Red Booklet inside my pocket. I placed the Red Booklet inside my pocket. I dropped the Book of Freedom inside my pocket. I closed my royal pocket. I smacked my royal horse. I smacked my white horse. I smacked my royal horse. I smacked my royal horse the third time. I saw something. I saw something happening. I saw something. I saw something strange. I saw something strange happening. I saw my royal horse. I saw my white horse. I saw my white horse running. I saw my royal horse running. I saw my white horse running faster. I saw my royal horse running faster. I saw my army horse. I saw my army horse riding faster and faster. I saw my white horse running past snowing woodlands. I was riding. I was riding forward. I was riding faster. I rode past raining woodlands. I rode past snowing woodlands. I rode past snowing mountains. I rode past snowing forest. I rode past snowing castles. I rode past snowing rivers. I rode past Hungarian women. I rode past Hungarian men. I rode past Hungarian soldiers. I rode past Hungarian cowboys. I rode past Hungarian creatures. I approached another tunnel. I approached another tunnel of darkness. I rode inside the tunnel. I rode inside the tunnel of darkness. I rode faster. I rode faster and faster. I rode faster than a warrior. I rode faster than a soldier. I rode inside the mysterious tunnel. I rode inside a warring tunnel. I rode faster. I rode faster and faster. I rode like a warrior. I rode like a royal warrior. I rode like a soldier. I rode like a royal soldier. I rode like a stranger. I rode like a royal stranger. I rode like a merchant soldier. I rode like a merchant warrior. I rode inside the tunnel of darkness. I rode faster. I rode faster and faster. I rode faster than a pirate boat. I approached someone. I approached another person. I approached my best friend. I approached my former friend. I approached the lion of Judah. I approached the lion king. I approached the king of Jerusalem. I approached my heavenly friend. I approached my heavenly lion. I approached him inside the tunnel. I approached him inside the mysterious tunnel. I approached him inside the strange tunnel. I approached him inside the tunnel of darkness. I saw my royal horse. I saw my horse running no more. I looked upwards. I saw the war veteran and his dragon. I saw them upwards. I saw them inside the tunnel. I saw them inside the tunnel of darkness. I saw them above the tunnel of darkness. I saw them upwards. I saw them flying no more. I saw the war veteran. I saw him sitting on his dragon. I saw him riding no more. I saw him flying no more. I saw him following no more. I saw the lion king. I saw my heavenly lion. I saw Leo. I saw him inside the tunnel. I saw him inside the tunnel of darkness. I saw the lion of Judah. I saw him speaking. I saw the lion king. I saw him welcoming me. I saw my heavenly lion. I saw him greeting me. I saw my lion friend. I saw him blessing me. I saw my heavenly lion. I saw him thanking me. I saw my heavenly lion. I saw him respecting me. I saw my lion protector. I saw him saluting me. I saw my friend lion. I saw him congratulating me. I saw my former friend. I saw him giving me thanks. I saw my heavenly lion. I saw him thanking me for coming farther. I looked at my best friend. I looked at my heavenly lion. I looked at Leo. I saw him waving goodbye. I saw him waving me goodbye. I saw him waving my heavenly protectors goodbye. I saw him waving the war veteran and his dragon goodbye. I saw something. I saw something happening. I saw something. I saw something strange. I saw something strange happening. I saw the lion of Judah. I saw the lion king. I saw my heavenly lion. I saw him disappearing. I saw him vanishing. I saw his disappearance. I smacked my royal horse. I smacked my white horse. I saw my horse running. I saw my horse running forward. I saw my horse running faster. I saw my horse running faster and faster. I saw my royal horse running. I saw my white horse inside the tunnel of darkness. I saw my horse running. I saw my horse running faster. I was sitting on my white horse. I was riding on my white horse. I rode faster. I rode faster and faster. I rode inside the tunnel of darkness. I rode forward. I rode faster. I rode outside the tunnel. I rode outside the tunnel of darkness. I rode inside another forest. I rode inside another snowing forest. I rode faster. I rode faster and faster. I rode past snowing woodlands. I rode past raining woodlands. I looked upwards. I saw my heavenly followers. I saw my heavenly protectors. I saw the war veteran and his dragon. I saw them protecting me and my horse. I saw them following me and my horse. I saw them flying upwards. I saw them flying inside snowing forest. I saw them flying above snowing woodlands. I saw them flying above heavenly trees. I saw them flying above snowing trees. I looked forward. I was riding. I was riding forward. I was riding faster. I rode past snowing trees. I rode past heavenly woodlands. I rode past snowing woodlands. I rode faster. I rode faster and faster. I rode past the snowing woodlands. I rode outside the snowing forest. I rode forward. I rode faster. I rode faster and faster. I rode faster than a warrior. I rode faster than a soldier. I rode past snowing rivers. I rode past snowing castles. I rode past snowing tunnels. I rode past snowing mountains. I rode faster. I rode faster and faster. I rode past warriors. I rode past soldiers. I rode past Hungarian soldiers. I rode past Hungarian warriors. I rode past Hungarian women. I rode past Hungarian men. I rode past Hungarian cowboys. I rode past Hungarian tractors. I rode past Hungarian war veterans. I rode faster. I rode faster and faster. I rode faster than a royal soldier. I rode faster than a pirate boat. I rode faster. I rode faster and faster. I was approaching somewhere. I was approaching another nation. I approached somewhere. I approached another nation.

CHAPTER 10

Prince Harry and His Journey From Hungary to Norway

I approached another nation. I approached another beautiful nation. I approached Norway. I was sitting on my horse. I kept riding. I kept riding like a royal warrior. I kept riding like a royal soldier. I kept riding as a royal soldier. I rode faster. I rode faster and faster. I continued riding. I continued riding faster. I continued riding faster and faster. I rode inside another snowing forest. I rode forward. I rode faster. I rode faster and faster. I rode past another snowing woodlands. I looked upwards. I saw my heavenly protectors. I saw my heavenly detectors. I saw my heavenly followers. I saw the war veteran and his dragon. I saw them flying forward. I saw them flying faster. I saw them flying faster and faster. I saw the war veteran. I saw him sitting on his dragon. I saw him riding on his mysterious dragon. I saw him riding forward. I saw him riding faster. I saw him riding faster and faster. I saw him riding above me and my horse. I saw him riding inside snowing forest. I saw him riding past snowing woodlands. I saw him riding above snowing woodlands. I saw him flying above snowing woodlands. I looked forward. I kept riding. I kept riding forward. I kept riding like a warrior. I kept riding like a royal warrior. I kept riding like a soldier. I kept riding like a royal soldier. I rode past snowing woodlands. I rode past snowing trees. I rode faster. I rode faster and faster. I rode faster than a warrior. I rode faster than a royal warrior. I rode inside another snowing forest. I rode forward. I rode faster. I rode faster and faster. I rode past snowing woodlands. I rode past snowing trees. I approached somewhere. I approached another snowing woodlands. I kept riding. I kept riding forward. I approached somewhere. I approached a beautiful river. I saw a beautiful river. I saw my horse. I saw my white horse. I saw my royal horse. I saw him running. I saw him running forward. I saw him running faster. I saw him running towards the river. I saw my royal horse. I saw my white horse. I saw my royal horse in front of the river. I looked upwards. I saw the sun set. I saw the dawn forest. I saw the dawn river. I saw the dawn woodlands. I saw the forest of darkness. I saw the river of darkness. I saw the woodlands of darkness. I looked above the snowing river. I saw the war veteran and his dragon. I saw them above the snowing river. I looked forward. I saw the snowing river. I saw my royal horse. I saw my horse running no more. I saw my horse in front of the river of darkness. I jumped off my horse. I jumped from my white horse. I grabbed my royal horse. I walked my royal horse. I walked my horse closer to the river. I splashed waters on my white horse. I washed my white horse. I washed my royal horse. I sat on the muddy floor. I felt the crispy cold wind. I felt the blowing wind. I felt relaxed. I felt warmed. I felt stronger. I felt magnified. I felt the snowing wind. I felt fearless. I felt magnetic. I felt crispy cold. I looked at my royal horse. I looked at my white horse. I saw him doing something. I saw him doing something strange. I saw him doing something mysterious. I saw him doing something heavenly. I saw my white horse. I saw my royal horse. I saw my horse drinking something. I saw my horse drinking water. I saw my horse drinking crispy cold water. I watched my heavenly horse. I watched my royal horse. I watched my white horse. I watched my horse drink water. I saw my horse drinking water. I saw my horse drinking water from the river of darkness. I watched my horse drink water. I watched until my horse finished drinking water. I saw everywhere in darkness. I saw darkness everywhere. I saw the river in darkness. I saw the dark river. I saw the river of darkness. Looked upwards. I looked above the river of darkness. I saw the war veteran and his dragon. I saw them flying downwards. I saw them on the snowing ground. I saw the dragon. I saw him on the ground. I saw the war veteran. I saw him sitting on his dragon. I saw him jumping off his dragon. I saw him sitting on the ground. I saw the war veteran. I saw him sitting behind me and my horse. He sat behind me and my royal horse. I saw his dragon. I saw his dragon sitting behind him. I saw the war veteran. I saw him sleeping. I saw his heavenly dragon. I saw him sleeping. I saw my white horse. I saw my royal horse. I saw him sleeping. I saw everyone sleeping. I saw everyone sleeping in darkness. I saw everyone. I saw everyone sleeping in front of the river. I felt the blowing river. I felt the blowing wind. I felt the blowing trees. I had a dream. I had a strange dream. I had a mysterious dream. I had a magical dream. I saw someone. I saw someone in my dream. I saw my best friend. I saw my heavenly friend. I saw the lion. I saw the lion of Judah. I saw the lion king. I saw Leo. I saw him welcoming me. I saw him respecting me. I saw him commanding me. I saw him protecting me. I saw him congratulating me. I saw him saluting me. I saw him congratulating me about my journey. I saw him congratulating me for coming farther. I saw him commanding me about my journey. I saw him commanding me to continue my journey. I saw him congratulating the war veteran and his dragon. I saw him congratulating them about their journey. I saw him congratulating them for coming farther. I saw the lion of Judah. I saw Leo. I saw him in my dream. I saw him in my strange dream. I saw him in my mysterious dream. I walked towards my heavenly lion. I walked in front of the lion of Judah. I did something. I did something great. I bowed downwards. I bowed my head downwards. I saluted him. I saluted my heavenly lion. I saw my heavenly lion. I saw him welcoming me. I saw him respecting me. I saw my heavenly lion. I saw him waving me goodbye. I saw him waving the war veteran goodbye. I saw him waving my horse goodbye. I saw him waving everyone goodbye. I saw something. I saw something happening. I saw something. I saw something strange. I saw something. I saw something strange happening. I saw my heavenly lion. I saw his disappearance. I saw him disappearing. I saw his vanishing. I saw him vanishing. I saw his existence no more. I felt the blowing river. I felt the crispy cold wind. I woke up the next morning. I saw the sun rising. I saw the sun rise. I saw lightness. I saw the river of lightness. I saw the snowing woodlands. I saw a snowing morning. I saw a snowing river. I saw a snowing forest. I looked around. I saw the war veteran and his dragon. I saw them awake in the snowing morning. I saw the war veteran. I saw him walking. I saw him walking forward. I saw him in front of the snowing river. I saw him drinking some water. I saw him turning around. I saw him walking forward. I saw him walking towards his heavenly dragon. I saw the war veteran. I saw him in front of his dragon. I saw him jumping on his dragon. I saw the war veteran. I saw him sitting on his dragon. I saw my white horse. I walked forward. I walked towards my white horse. I jumped onto my royal horse. I sat on my white horse. I saw my royal horse. I saw my horse turning around. I saw my horse running. I saw my horse running forward. I saw my horse running behind the snowing river. I saw my horse running faster. I saw my horse running faster and faster. I turned around. I saw the war veteran and his dragon. I saw them flying forward. I saw them flying above snowing forest. I saw them flying inside snowing forest. I saw them flying above the snowing river. I saw them flying above snowing woodlands. I saw the war veteran and his dragon. I saw them flying forward. I saw them flying faster. I saw them flying faster and faster. I saw them over speeding. I saw them flying above the snowing river. I saw the war veteran. I saw him riding on his dragon. I saw him riding forward. I saw him riding faster. I saw him riding faster and faster. I saw him flying on his heavenly dragon. I saw him flying faster. I saw him flying faster and faster. I saw him over speeding. I saw him flying above the snowing river. I saw him flying above the snowing woodlands. I saw him flying above the snowing forest. I was riding on my royal horse. I was riding forward. I rode forward. I rode inside the snowing forest. I rode past the snowing river. I rode past the snowing woodlands. I rode faster. I rode faster and faster. I rode faster than a royal soldier. I rode like a royal soldier. I rode like a royal warrior. I rode as fast as a royal soldier. I rode like a warrior rider. I rode faster and faster. I rode faster than a pirate warrior. I rode faster than a pirate boat. I rode past snowing woodlands. I rode past snowing rivers. I approached somewhere. I approached another snowing forest. I rode faster. I rode faster inside the snowing forest. I rode past another snowing woodlands. I rode forward. I rode faster and faster. I approached someone. I approached another friend. I approached another old man. I approached a white man. I saw him sitting on his black horse. I looked at his neck. I saw something. I saw something religious. I saw the white man. I saw the old man. I saw him wearing something. I saw him wearing a white necklace. I saw him wearing a sacred necklace. I saw the white man. I saw the old man. I saw him wearing a red jacket. I saw him wearing a large jacket. I saw him wearing a red round hat. I saw his black horse. I saw his horse behind me. I saw him looking at me. I saw the white old man. I saw him welcoming me. He welcomed me to Norway. I saw him asking for my name and country. He asked for my name and background. I told him about my background. I told him about my country. I told him about my name. I told him I was the prince of England. I told him I was Prince Harry. I told him I was from a royal family. I saw the old man. I saw the white old man. I saw him saluting me. I saw him behind me. I saw him looking at me. I saw him smiling. I saw looked at his necklace. I saw his sacred necklace. I asked him about his necklace. I asked him if he was a religious person. He told me he was a very religious person. He told me he was the reverend of Norway. I asked him why he appeared in the snowing woodlands. He told me he was patrolling the snowing woodlands. I asked him why he was patrolling the snowing woodlands. He replied me with smiles. He replied me it was for his protection. He replied me it was for spiritual protection. He replied me smiling. He told me it was because of witches and wizards. I asked him a question. I asked him if he was a reverend. He replied me with smiles. He told me he was the reverend of Norway. He told me he was also reverend of the snowing forest. He replied me smiling. I looked at the reverend of Norway. I asked for his name. He replied me with smiles. He replied me smiling. He told me about his name. He told me he was called Reverend Norman. He replied me with smiles. He replied me smiling. I saw the reverend of Norway. I met the reverend inside the snowing forest. I met the reverend of the snowing woodlands. I looked at the old man. I looked at the reverend. I looked at Reverend Norman. I saw him smiling. I smiled with him. I saw the reverend. I saw the religious man. I saw him reaching for my hand. I saw him shaking my hand. I saw him praying. I saw him praying for me. I saw Reverend Norman. I saw my religious friend. I saw him raising his hands upwards. I looked upwards. I saw him praying. I saw him praying for the war veteran and his dragon. I looked at the reverend of Norway. I saw him doing something. I saw him doing something spiritual. I saw him doing something religious. I saw him doing something miraculous. I saw him waving prayers. He waved prayers. I looked at the reverend of the snowing woodlands. I saw him blessing me. I saw him blessing the war veteran and his dragon. I saw Reverend Norman. I saw him removing his necklace. I saw him removing his religious necklace. I saw him handing me his religious necklace. I reached my hands forward. I grabbed his religious necklace. I looked at the reverend. I saw him bowing his head. I placed his religious necklace onto my neck. I looked at the reverend. I saw him looking at me. I saw him smiling. I saw him talking. I saw him talking about the religious necklace. He told me something about the religious necklace. He told me it was a victorious necklace. He told me it was a necklace of victory. He told me it was a glorious necklace. He told me it was a necklace of glory. I saw the reverend of the snowing forest. I saw the reverend in the snowing woodlands. I saw Reverend Norman. I saw him shaking my hands. I saw him smiling. I saw him waving goodbye. I saw him waving me and my horse goodbye. I saw him waving the war veteran and his dragon goodbye. I saw the reverend of Norway. I saw the reverend inside the snowing forest. I saw the reverend of the snowing woodlands. I saw Reverend Norman. I saw him smacking his black horse. I saw him smacking his black horse again. I saw him smacking his horse the third time. I saw his black horse. I saw his holy horse. I saw the reverend and his horse behind me. I saw his horse running. I saw his horse running forward. I saw his horse running faster. I smacked my horse. I saw my horse running. I saw my horse running faster. I rode outside the snowing woodlands. I rode past rivers. I rode past forest. I rode past castles. I rode past tunnels. I rode farther. I approached another nation.

CHAPTER 11

Prince Harry and His Journey From Norway to Albania

I rode farther and farther. I approached somewhere. I approached another world. I approached another beautiful world. I approached another beautiful nation. I approached another Romantic nation. I approached Albania. I rode past snowing buildings. I rode past snowing rivers. I rode past heavenly mountains. I rode past snowing mountains. I rode faster. I rode faster and faster. I kept riding. I kept riding forward. I rode past veterans. I rode past soldiers. I rode past old soldiers. I rode past snowing waters. I rode on snowing waters. I rode on muddy waters. I rode faster and faster. I rode past Albanian mountains. I rode past Albanian rivers. I rode past Albanian castles. I rode faster. I rode on my royal horse. I rode faster on my white horse. I rode faster than a warrior. I rode faster than a soldier. I kept riding. I kept riding forward. I kept riding like a warrior. I kept riding like a soldier. I rode faster. I rode faster and faster. I approached another tunnel. I approached another snowing tunnel. I rode inside the snowing tunnel. I saw the tunnel of darkness. I rode inside the tunnel of darkness. I rode faster. I rode faster and faster. I saw the tunnel of darkness. I rode faster. I rode faster and faster. I kept riding. I kept riding forward. I rode like a warrior. I rode like a soldier. I rode like a royal soldier. I rode like a royal warrior. I rode inside the tunnel of darkness. I continued riding. I continued riding forward. I continued riding faster. I continued riding faster and faster. I approached someone. I approached someone inside the tunnel. I saw someone inside the tunnel of darkness. I saw someone appearing. I saw someone appearing in front of me. I saw my best friend. I saw my heavenly lion. I saw Leo. I saw him appearing. I saw him appearing in front of me. I saw him in front of me. I saw him inside the tunnel of darkness. I saw him in front of me and my white horse. I saw him in front of the war veteran and his dragon. I saw my protector. I saw my heavenly lion. I saw him speaking. I saw him welcoming me. He welcomed me to Albania. I saw him welcoming the war veteran and his dragon. He welcomed them to Albania. I saw the heavenly lion. I saw him congratulating me. I saw him congratulating me about my journey. He congratulated me for coming farther. I saw my heavenly lion. I saw him congratulating the war veteran and his dragon. He congratulated them about their journey. He congratulated them for coming farther. I saw my protector. I saw my heavenly lion. I bowed my head downwards. I saluted my protector. I saluted my heavenly lion. I turned around. I saw the war veteran and his dragon. I saw their head downwards. I saw them saluting the heavenly lion. I saw my protector. I saw my heavenly lion. I saw him respecting me. I saw him respecting the war veteran and his dragon. I turned around. I looked forward. I looked at my protector. I looked at my heavenly lion. I saw him blessing me and my horse. I saw him blessing the war veteran and his dragon. I saw my heavenly lion. I saw him praying. I saw him waving prayers. I saw him mentioning the Lord's Prayer. I looked at my heavenly lion. I saw something. I saw something happening. I saw something strange. I saw something strange happening. I saw my heavenly lion. I saw him vanishing. I saw him disappearing. I saw his disappearance. I saw his existence no more. I saw his appearance no more. I saw the vanishing of my protector. I saw the vanishing of my heavenly lion. I smacked my white horse. I smacked my royal horse. I smacked my horse for the third time. I saw my royal horse. I saw my horse running. I saw my horse running faster. I saw my horse running faster and faster. I was riding on my horse. I rode faster. I rode faster and faster. I rode inside the tunnel. I rode inside the tunnel of darkness. I rode forward. I looked upwards. I looked above the tunnel. I saw the war veteran and his dragon. I saw them in front of me. I saw them ahead of me. I saw them farther way. I saw them flying. I saw them flying faster. I saw the war veteran. I saw him riding on his dragon. I saw him riding forward. I saw him riding faster. I saw him riding faster than me. I saw the war veteran. I saw the flying veteran. I saw him flying above the tunnel. I saw him flying on his dragon. I saw him flying forward. I saw him flying like a warrior. I saw him flying above the tunnel of darkness. I looked forward. I smacked my white horse. I smacked my royal horse. I saw something. I saw something happening. I saw my royal horse. I saw my white horse. I saw my running horse. I saw my horse running. I saw my horse running faster. I saw my horse running faster and faster. I saw my horse over speeding. I saw my horse running like a warrior. I saw my horse running like a royal warrior. I saw my horse running like a royal soldier. I saw my horse running. I saw my horse running outside the tunnel. I saw my horse running outside the tunnel of darkness. I saw my horse running. I looked upwards. I saw the war veteran and his dragon. I saw them behind me. I saw them flying. I saw them following me and my horse. I saw my horse running. I saw my horse running forward. I saw my horse running faster. I saw my horse running faster and faster. I saw my horse running past another snowing rivers. I saw my horse running past another snowing mountains. I saw my horse running past other snowing tunnels. I saw my horse running past another snowing castles. I looked forward. I saw somewhere. I saw another world. I saw another snowing world. I saw another snowing forest. I saw my white horse. I saw my royal horse. I saw my running horse. I saw my horse running towards somewhere. I saw my horse running towards another snowing forest. I saw my running horse. I saw my horse running. I saw my horse running faster. I saw my horse running. I saw my horse entering another snowing forest. I saw my horse inside another snowing forest. I was sitting on my horse. I was riding on my horse. I rode inside a snowing forest. I rode faster. I rode faster and faster. I rode faster than a snowing warrior. I rode faster and faster. I rode faster like a royal warrior. I rode past snowing woodlands. I rode on muddy grounds. I rode on snowing grounds. I kept riding. I kept riding forward. I kept riding like a warrior. I kept riding like a royal warrior. I kept riding like a royal soldier. I approached someone. I approached an old man. I saw a white old man. I saw him wearing a large black hoodie. I saw him sitting on his brown horse. I saw him having a lot of facial hair. I saw him in front of me. I saw him welcoming me. I saw him smiling. I saw him asking for my name. I replied him I was Harry. I replied him I was a prince from England. I replied him I was the prince of England. I looked at him. I saw him looking at me. I saw him smiling. I saw him reaching his hands forward. I saw him shaking my hands. I shook his hands. I saw him smiling. I looked at him. I started smiling. He saw me smiling. He welcomed me to Albania. I looked at the old man. I looked at the Albanian old man. I asked for his name. He replied me smiling. He replied me with heavy smiles. He replied me he was a philosopher. He replied me his name was Christopher. He replied me he was called Christopher. I asked him a question. I asked him where he was travelling towards. He replied me he was not a traveller. He replied me he was a philosopher. He replied me he was an observer. He replied me he was observing the snowing woodlands. He replied me he was enjoying a ride inside the snowing forest. He replied me he does that every day. He replied me he was observing the singing birds. He replied me he was observing the blowing wind. He replied me he was riding. He replied me he was having a ride on his brown horse. He replied me he was having a ride. He replied me he was admiring the beautiful forest. I saw the old man. I saw the philosopher. I saw the philosopher of Albania. I saw Christopher. I saw him sitting on his brown horse. I saw him and his brown horse. I saw them behind me. I saw the philosopher.

I saw Christopher. I saw his hands inside his pocket. I saw him removing something. I saw him pulling out something. I saw him pulling out a diamond ring. I saw him holding a diamond ring. I saw him reaching for my hands. I reached my hands forward. I saw Christopher. I saw the philosopher. I saw him putting the diamond ring on my finger. I looked at the diamond ring. I looked at Christopher. I asked him a question. I asked him about the diamond ring. I asked him the purpose of the diamond ring. He replied me the diamond ring was for victory of my journey. I looked at Christopher. I saw him smiling. I saw him saluting me. I saw him wishing me a good luck journey. I saw Christopher. I saw him wishing the war veteran and his dragon a good luck journey. I saw the philosopher of Albania. I saw him waving me goodbye. I saw him waving the war veteran and his dragon goodbye. I saw Christopher. I saw the philosopher of Albania. I saw him smacking his brown horse. I saw him smacking his brown horse again. I saw him smacking his brown horse the third time. I saw Christopher. I saw the philosopher of Albania. I saw him riding. I saw him riding forward. I saw him riding farther. I smacked my white horse. I smacked my royal horse. I smacked my horse the third time. I saw my white horse. I saw him running. I saw him running forward. I saw him running faster. I saw him running past snowing woodlands. I looked upwards. I looked above the snowing woodlands. I saw the war veteran and his dragon. I saw them flying behind me. I looked forward. I saw my horse running. I saw my horse running faster. I saw my horse running faster and faster. I saw my horse running farther. I saw me and my horse outside the snowing woodlands. I saw me and my horse outside the snowing forest. I rode on my royal horse. I rode forward. I rode faster. I rode faster and faster. I rode faster than a royal warrior. I rode faster than a royal soldier. I rode faster like a royal warrior. I rode faster like a royal soldier. I rode past another snowing river. I rode past snowing mountains. I rode past snowing tunnels. I rode past the snowing forest. I approached somewhere. I approached another world.

CHAPTER 12

Prince Harry and His Journey From Albania to South Africa

I approached another nation. I approached another beautiful nation. I approached South Africa. I rode inside South Africa. I rode on my white horse. I rode inside South Africa. I looked upwards. I saw the war veteran and his dragon. I saw them above the heavenly mountains. I saw them above me. I saw them behind me. I saw them flying. I saw them flying forward. I saw them following. I saw them following me and my white horse. I saw them flying above the South African mountains. I rode past South African Mountains. I rode past snowing mountains. I rode past royal castles. I rode past snowing castles. I rode past the castles of South Africa. I rode past South African rivers. I rode past snowing rivers. I rode past another snowing river. I rode past raining rivers. I rode past another raining river. I rode past the rivers of South Africa. I rode past the snowing rivers of South Africa. I rode past mountains. I rode past South African mountains. I rode past snowing mountains. I rode past raining mountains. I rode past the mountains of South Africa. I rode past the snowing mountains of South Africa. I rode past the raining mountains of South Africa. I approached somewhere. I approached another tunnel. I approached another tunnel of darkness. I approached a South African tunnel. I rode inside the tunnel. I rode inside the tunnel of darkness. I rode forward. I rode faster. I rode faster and faster. I rode faster like a royal warrior. I rode faster like a royal soldier. I rode faster and faster. I rode inside a mysterious tunnel. I approached somewhere. I approached another friend. I saw my white horse. I saw my horse running no more. I looked upwards. I looked above the heavenly tunnel. I saw the war veteran and his dragon. I saw them flying no more. I saw them above the heavenly tunnel. I saw my horse in front of someone. I saw something. I saw something happening. I saw something strange. I saw something strange happening. I looked forward. I saw someone appearing. I saw someone in front of me. I saw a giant dragon in front of me. I saw a mysterious Dragon. I saw a massive black Dragon. I saw a giant dragon. I saw the giant black dragon. I saw him talking. I saw him talking to me. I saw him talking to the war veteran and his dragon. I heard something. I heard the black dragon speaking. I heard the dragon welcoming me and my royal horse. I heard the dragon welcoming me and my horse to South Africa. I saw the dragon welcoming me and my white horse. I saw the dragon welcoming me and my horse to South Africa. I heard the strange dragon. I heard the giant dragon. I heard the mysterious dragon. I heard the dragon welcoming the war veteran and his dragon. I heard the dragon welcoming them to South Africa. I saw the strange dragon. I saw the dragon welcoming the war veteran and his dragon. I saw the dragon welcoming them to South Africa. I saw the giant dragon. I saw something. I saw something strange. I saw something mysterious. I saw something strange happening. I saw something mysterious happening. I saw the giant dragon. I saw the mysterious dragon. I saw the strange dragon. I saw the dragon of South Africa. I saw the dragon doing something. I saw the dragon opening his giant mouth. I saw the dragon blowing out strange fire. I saw the dragon blowing out aggressive fire. I saw the dragon blowing out blue fire. I saw the dragon blowing out heavy blue fire. I looked forward. I looked at the dragon. I saw the dragon. I saw him blowing out aggressive fire no more. I saw him blowing out strange fire no more. I felt something. I felt something after the dragon blew out his heavy fire. I felt welcomed. I felt magnetic. I felt stronger. I felt heavier. I felt heavenly. I felt warmer. I felt like a warrior. I felt like a royal warrior. I felt like a soldier. I felt like a royal soldier. I felt magnificent. I felt a stranger no more. I looked at the giant dragon. I looked at the dragon of South Africa. I saw something. I saw him doing something. I saw the mysterious dragon. I saw the giant dragon. I saw the strange dragon. I saw him laughing. I saw him smiling. I saw him welcoming me. I saw his head downwards. I saw him saluting me. I saw him respecting me. I saw the giant dragon. I saw him speaking. I saw him speaking about my journey. I saw him congratulating me. I saw him congratulating me about my journey. I saw him congratulating me for coming farther. I saw the giant dragon. I saw him waving me and my horse goodbye. I saw him waving the war veteran and his dragon goodbye. I looked at the giant dragon. I looked at the dragon of South Africa. I saw something. I saw something happening. I saw the giant dragon. I saw him opening his mouth. I saw him blowing out something. I saw him blowing out something again. I saw him blowing out another fire. I saw him blowing out another blue fire. I saw him blowing another aggressive fire. I saw the giant dragon. I saw the dragon of South Africa. I saw him flapping his mighty wings. I saw him flying. I saw him flying above the tunnel. I saw him flying forward. I saw him flying above me and my horse. I saw him flying above the war veteran and his dragon. I turned around. I looked upwards. I looked above the heavenly tunnel. I saw something. I saw something happening. I saw the giant dragon. I saw the strange dragon. I saw the dragon of South Africa. I saw him disappearing. I saw his disappearance. I saw him appearing no more. I saw him vanishing. I saw his vanishing. I saw him no more. I turned around. I looked forward. I smacked my horse. I smacked my royal horse. I smacked my white horse. I saw my horse running. I saw my horse running forward. I saw my horse running faster. I saw my horse running faster and faster. I rode on my white horse. I rode faster. I rode faster and faster. I rode like a pirate boat. I rode like a pirate warrior. I rode like a pirate soldier. I rode inside the tunnel of darkness. I rode faster, faster and faster. I rode outside the tunnel. I rode outside the tunnel of darkness. I rode past tunnels. I rode past another tunnel. I rode past castles. I rode past another castle. I rode past rivers. I rode past another river. I rode inside another forest. I rode inside another snowing woodlands. I rode past snowing woodlands. I rode past another snowing woodlands. I rode past muddy woodlands. I rode faster inside muddy woodlands. I continued riding. I continued riding forward. I continued riding faster. I kept riding. I kept riding forward. I continued riding faster. I rode faster. I rode faster inside the snowing woodlands. I rode faster inside the South African woodlands. I rode past snowing woodlands. I rode faster and faster. I looked upwards. I saw the war veteran and his dragon. I saw them above the snowing woodlands. I saw them flying. I saw them flying above the South African woodlands. I saw them flying forward. I saw them flying faster. I saw them upwards. I saw them flying faster. I saw them ahead of me and my running horse. I saw my running horse. I saw my horse running faster. I saw my horse running faster and faster. I saw my horse speeding. I saw my horse over speeding. I rode on my running horse. I rode inside another snowing forest. I rode past snowing woodlands. I rode faster. I rode faster and faster. I rode faster like a royal prince. I rode faster like a royal warrior. I rode faster like a royal soldier. I approached somewhere. I approached another river. I approached another South African river. I saw my horse running no more. I saw me and my horse. I was in front of the South African river. I saw a white woman. I saw a white old woman. I saw her near the river. I saw her kneeling downwards. I saw her in front of the river. I saw her wearing a massive black hoodie. I saw her talking. I saw her speaking. I saw her talking about human flesh. I heard the old woman. I heard her talking. I heard echoes of her blasted crescendos. I saw the old woman. I saw her doing something. I saw her turning around. I saw her looking at me and my royal horse. I saw her walking. I saw her walking forward. I saw her walking towards me. I saw the old woman. I saw her in front of me. I saw her holding a cup. I looked at her. I saw her strange fingers. I saw her long fingers. I saw her fingers looking like lion claws. I heard her talking. I heard her speaking to me. I saw her welcoming me. I saw her welcoming the war veteran and his dragon. I saw her smiling. I saw her laughing. I saw her holding a black cup. I saw her looking inside the cup. I saw her eyes rolling. I saw her blue eyes. I saw something. I saw something happening. I saw something strange happening. I saw the old woman. I saw her blue eyes. I saw her eyes rolling. I saw her eyes turning red. I saw her handing me the cup. I grabbed the cup. I looked inside the cup. I saw nothing inside the cup. I saw something. I saw something strange. I saw something strange happening. I saw the empty cup. I saw the appearance of boiling water. I saw boiling water appear inside the cup. I looked at the old woman. I saw her knocking her head. I drank the boiling water. I felt magnetic. I felt like a warrior. I felt like a soldier. I felt stronger. I felt like a soldier. I felt energetic. I looked at the old woman. I saw her looking at me. I asked for her name. She replied me softly. She replied me she was called Ruth Linda. She replied me she was an old witch. She replied me she was a former war woman. She asked for my name. I replied her I was a prince. I replied her I was the prince of England. I saw her talking. I saw her welcoming me. I saw her welcoming the war veteran and his dragon. I saw her blessing me and my horse. I saw her blessing the war veteran and his dragon. I saw the witch of the South African snowing forest. I saw her speaking words of magic. I saw her blessing everyone. I gave her cup back to her. I saw her smiling. I saw her laughing. I heard echoes of her blasted smiles. I heard echoes of her blasted magic. I looked at the white old woman. I looked at the witch. I saw her looking at me. I saw her reaching her hands forward. I saw her shaking my hands. She shook my hands. I felt warmer. I felt stronger. I felt heavier. I felt miraculous. I felt magical. I felt like a warrior. I felt like a royal warrior. I felt magnetic. I felt magnificent. I looked at the old woman. I looked at the witch. I saw her praying. I saw her praying for me. I saw her waving prayers. I saw her waving for magical prayers. I saw her waving for miraculous prayers. I saw her mentioning the Lord's Prayer. I saw the old woman. I saw the old witch. I saw her looking at me. I saw her waving me goodbye. I saw her waving the war veteran and his dragon goodbye. I saw something. I saw something happening. I saw something strange. I saw something strange happening. I saw the old woman. I saw the old witch. I saw the witch of the snowing river. I saw the witch of the snowing forest. I saw the witch of the snowing woodlands. I saw the witch of the South African forest. I saw her doing something. I saw her doing something strange. I saw her doing something magical. I saw her doing something miraculous. I saw her vanishing. I saw her disappearing. I saw her existence no more. I saw her appearance no more. I saw her vanished into the air. I looked forward. I smacked my white horse. I smacked my royal horse. I saw my horse running. I saw my horse running forwards. I saw my horse running faster. I saw my horse running faster and faster. I saw my horse running past the river. I saw my horse running past the snowing river. I saw my horse running past the snowing woodlands. I saw my horse running faster. I was riding. I was riding on my white horse. I rode faster. I rode faster and faster. I rode inside the snowing forest. I rode inside the South African forest. I rode faster. I rode faster and faster. I rode faster than a warrior. I rode faster than a soldier. I rode faster, faster and faster. I rode outside the snowing forest. I rode outside the snowing woodlands. I rode outside the snowing rivers. I rode past South African mountains. I rode past snowing mountains. I looked upwards. I saw the war veteran and his dragon. I saw them ahead of me. I saw them flying. I saw them flying above the mountains. I looked forward. I rode faster. I rode faster and faster. I rode past South African women. I rode past soldiers. I rode past warriors. I rode past cowboys. I rode past rivers. I rode past merchants. I rode past pirates. I rode past tunnels. I rode past castles. I rode past safari parks. I rode faster. I rode faster and faster. I rode faster than a warrior. I rode faster than a merchant. I rode faster than a pirate. I rode faster than a cowboy. I rode faster and farther. I approached somewhere. I approached another nation.

CHAPTER 13

Prince Harry and His Journey From South Africa to Egypt

I approached another nation. I approached another desert. I approached another beautiful nation. I approached Egypt. I rode faster. I rode faster and faster. I rode like a warrior. I approached somewhere. I approached another beautiful desert. I approached another mysterious desert. I approached the Sahara desert. I rode past dusty desert. I rode on dusty desert. I rode forward. I rode faster and faster. I saw beautiful camels. I saw women riding on camels. I saw men riding on camels. I rode faster. I rode faster and faster. I rode past warriors. I rode past soldiers. I rode like a royal solider. I rode forward. I rode faster. I rode faster and faster. I looked upwards. I looked above the heavenly sky. I saw the war veteran and his dragon. I saw them ahead of me. I saw them flying. I saw them flying above the Egyptian desert. I saw the war veteran and his dragon. I saw them ahead of me. I looked forward. I saw warriors. I saw warriors riding on their camels. I rode forward. I rode faster. I rode faster and faster. I rode on Egyptian deserts. I rode on muddy deserts. I rode faster. I rode faster and faster. I approached someone. I approached a former friend. I approached a dragon. I approached a giant black dragon. I approached another giant dragon. I saw the giant dragon. I saw him in front of me. I saw him doing something. I saw him opening his mouth. I saw something. I saw something strange. I saw something happening. I saw something strange happening. I saw the giant dragon. I saw him blowing out blue fire. I saw something.

I saw something strange. I saw something happening. I saw something strange happening. I saw the moving deserts. I saw the blowing deserts. I saw the windy deserts. I saw the vanishing desert. I saw everything back to normal. I looked forward. I looked at the giant dragon. I heard him speaking. I saw him talking. I saw him welcoming me. I heard him welcoming me. I heard him welcoming me to Egypt. I saw him welcoming me to Egypt. I saw the giant dragon. I saw him speaking about my successful journey. I saw him congratulating me about my journey. I saw him congratulating me for coming farther. I saw the giant dragon. I saw him welcoming the war veteran and his dragon. I was sitting on my white horse. I bowed my head downwards. I saluted the dragon. I saluted the giant dragon. I respected the giant dragon. I saw the giant dragon. I saw the black dragon. I saw my former friend. I saw him smiling. I saw him respecting me. I saw the dragon. I saw him opening his mouth. I saw him blowing out blue fire. I saw something. I saw something happening. I saw something. I saw something strange. I saw something strange happening. I saw the moving deserts. I saw the blowing deserts. I saw the blowing wind. I saw the vanishing desert. I saw something. I saw something happening. I saw everything coming back to normal. I saw the desert blowing no more. I saw the wind blowing no more. I saw the dragon. I saw the giant dragon. I saw him doing something. I saw him flapping his mighty wings. I saw the giant dragon. I saw him flying upwards. I saw him above the Egyptian desert. I saw him flying forward. I saw him vanishing. I saw him vanished above the desert sky. I looked forward. I reached for my hands. I reached my hands inside my pocket. I removed something. I removed something precious. I removed something special. I removed the Red Booklet. I removed the Book of Freedom. I opened the Red Booklet. I opened the Book of Freedom. I looked inside the Red Booklet. I looked inside the Book of Freedom. I saw something. I saw something happening. I saw something mysterious. I saw something mysterious happening.

I saw two warring nations. I saw two fighting nations. I saw two nations at war. I saw fighting soldiers. I saw Australian soldiers. I saw fighting Australian soldiers. I saw Sri Lankan soldiers. I saw fighting Sri Lankan soldiers. I saw dead Australian soldiers. I saw dead Sri Lankan soldiers. I saw damaged buildings. I saw bombardments of buildings. I saw smoke everywhere. I was emotionless. I shook my head in disbelief. I closed the Red Booklet. I placed it inside my pocket. I smacked my white horse. I smacked my royal horse. I smacked my horse again. I saw my horse running. I saw my horse running forward. I saw my horse running faster. I saw my horse running faster and faster. I looked upwards. I looked above the desert sky. I saw the war veteran and his dragon. I saw them above the heavenly sky. I saw them above the desert sky. I saw them flying. I saw them flying above the desert sky. I saw them ahead of me and my horse. I looked forward. I was riding forward. I was riding on my white horse. I rode on muddy deserts. I rode on windy deserts. I rode on Egyptian deserts. I rode faster. I rode faster and faster. I rode like a royal warrior. I rode like a royal soldier. I rode like a super hero. I rode past warriors. I rode past Egyptian warriors. I rode past Egyptian camels. I rode like a legend. I rode like a pirate warrior. I rode like a pirate rider. I rode on my royal horse. I rode on my white horse. I rode on my running horse. I rode faster. I rode faster and faster. I kept riding. I kept riding forward. I kept riding. I continued riding faster. I rode faster and faster. I approached someone. I approached my lion friend. I approached Leo. I saw my white horse. I saw my horse running no more. I saw my horse in front of my lion friend. I saw my heavenly lion. I saw him behind me and my horse. I saw him welcoming me. I saw him welcoming the war veteran and his dragon. I saw him speaking. I saw him speaking about my journey. I saw him congratulating me. I saw him congratulating me for travelling farther. I saw him congratulating the war veteran and his dragon. I saw him congratulating them for travelling farther. I saw my lion friend. I saw him blessing me. I saw my lion friend.

I saw him blessing the war veteran and his dragon. I saw my lion friend. I saw him waving me goodbye. I saw my lion friend. I saw him waving the war veteran and his dragon goodbye. I saw my lion friend. I saw him praying. I saw him praying for me. I saw him praying for the war veteran and his dragon. I saw my heavenly lion. I saw him mentioning the Lord's Prayer. I saw the heavenly lion. I saw Leo. I saw something. I saw something happening. I saw my lion friend. I saw him vanishing. I saw him disappearing. I saw his disappearance. I saw his existence no more. I looked forward. I smacked my royal horse. I smacked my white horse. I smacked my horse again. I saw my horse running. I saw my horse running faster. I saw my horse running faster and faster. I saw my horse running faster like a warrior. I saw my horse running on Egyptian deserts. I saw my horse riding past Egyptian veterans. I was riding on my white horse. I rode on my running horse. I rode with my head downwards. I rode faster. I rode faster and faster. I rode past Egyptian soldiers. I rode on Egyptian deserts. I rode farther. I rode faster and faster. I rode faster and farther. I rode farther and farther. I rode past Egyptian cowboys. I rode past Egyptian rivers. I rode past Egyptian mountains. I rode past Egyptian knights. I rode faster. I felt the blowing desert. I felt the blowing wind. I felt the warmed desert. I felt like an Egyptian soldier. I felt like the prince of Egypt. I rode faster. I rode faster and faster. I rode like a royal warrior. I rode like a royal soldier. I rode like a royal prince. I rode forward. I rode with my head downwards. I rode faster. I rode faster and faster. I rode faster than a warrior. I rode faster than a soldier. I rode faster. I rode faster and faster. I rode faster and farther. I rode farther and farther. I approached somewhere. I approached somewhere beautiful. I approached another nation.

CHAPTER 14

Prince Harry and His Journey From Egypt to Algeria

I approached another nation. I approached another African nation. I approached another Northern African nation. I approached Algeria. I rode on my royal horse. I rode on my white horse. I rode forward. I rode faster. I rode faster and faster. I rode faster than a warrior. I rode on a muddy desert. I rode on a windy desert. I rode on my royal horse. I rode with my head downwards. I rode faster. I rode faster and faster. I rode past Algerian mountains. I rode past Algerian rivers. I rode past Algerian soldiers. I rode past Algerian camels. I rode faster. I rode faster than a rollercoaster. I rode faster and faster. I rode faster like a royal soldier. I kept riding. I kept riding forward. I kept riding on muddy desert. I kept riding on windy desert. I continued riding. I continued riding forward. I continued riding faster. I continued riding faster and faster. I continued riding faster than a royal warrior. I continued riding like a royal warrior. I continued riding on windy desert. I continued riding on muddy desert. I felt the blowing wind. I felt warmer. I felt hotter. I felt the muddy dirt. I felt the blowing muds. I felt like a royal rider. I felt stronger. I felt magnificent. I felt like a pirate rider. I felt like a pirate warrior. I felt like a pirate soldier. I felt magnetic. I felt happier. I felt energetic. I felt like a merchant sailor. I felt like a pirate boat rider. I rode on my white horse. I rode forward. I rode on muddy dirt. I rode on windy dirt. I rode faster. I rode faster and faster. I rode faster like a royal prince. I rode faster like a royal soldier.

I rode faster like a royal warrior. I kept riding on my royal horse. I kept riding forward. I kept riding. I kept riding like a merchant rider. I approached a dragon. I approached a former friend. I approached my dragon friend. I saw my white horse. I saw my royal horse. I saw my horse running no more. I saw my royal horse. I saw my horse in front of a giant dragon. I saw my horse in front of my former friend. I saw my former dragon. I saw him in front of me and my horse. I saw the giant black dragon. I saw him opening his mighty mouth. I saw my former friend. I saw the giant dragon. I saw him doing something. I saw him doing something strange. I saw him doing something mysterious. I saw him doing something magical. I saw something. I saw something strange. I saw something strange happening. I saw something mysterious happening. I saw the giant dragon. I saw him blowing out red fire. I saw something. I saw something happening. I saw the blowing wind. I saw the blowing dirt. I felt the blowing wind. I felt the muddy wind. I felt the moving desert. I felt hotter. I felt warmer. I felt stronger. I felt magnetic. I felt energetic. I felt overwhelmed. I felt crispy cold no more. I felt like a royal hero. I felt like a royal super hero. I felt like a royal soldier. I felt like a royal warrior. I felt warmer. I felt hotter. I felt cold no more. I looked forward. I looked at the giant dragon. I saw him speaking. I saw the giant dragon. I saw him welcoming me and my horse. I saw him welcoming the war veteran and his dragon. I saw the giant dragon. I saw my dragon friend. I saw him speaking. I saw him speaking about my journey. I saw him speaking about the war veteran and his dragon journey. I saw the giant dragon. I saw him congratulating me and my horse for coming farther. I saw the giant dragon. I saw him congratulating the war veteran and his dragon for coming farther. I looked forward. I looked at the giant dragon. I was sitting on my horse. I bowed my head downwards. I saluted the giant dragon. I respected the giant dragon. I saw the war veteran. I saw him sitting on his dragon. I saw his head downwards. I saw him saluting the giant dragon. I saw him respecting the giant dragon. I looked forward. I saw the giant dragon. I saw his head downwards. I saw him saluting me and my horse. I saw him respecting me and my horse. I saw him saluting the war veteran and his dragon. I saw him respecting the war veteran and his dragon. I saw the giant dragon. I saw him smiling. I saw him blessing me and my horse. I saw him blessing the war veteran and his dragon. I saw the giant dragon. I saw him praying. I saw him praying for me and my horse. I saw him praying for the war veteran and his dragon. I saw the strange dragon. I saw the mysterious dragon. I saw the giant dragon. I saw him doing something. I saw him doing something heavenly. I saw I saw him mentioning the Lord's Prayer. I saw the giant dragon. I saw him smiling. I saw the giant dragon. I saw him waving me goodbye. I saw him waving the war veteran and his dragon goodbye. I looked forward. I looked at the giant dragon. I saw the giant dragon. I saw him doing something. I saw him doing something strange. I saw him doing something mysterious. I saw the giant dragon. I saw him flapping his mighty wings. I saw the giant dragon. I saw him rising. I saw him rising upwards. I saw the giant dragon. I saw him upwards. I saw the heavenly dragon. I saw him upwards. I saw him above the Algerian desert. I saw the giant dragon. I saw him above the Algerian sky. I saw him flying. I saw him flying forward. I saw the giant dragon. I saw him flying faster. I saw him flying faster and faster. I saw the giant dragon. I saw him vanishing. I saw him vanished above the desert sky. I saw him disappearing. I saw him disappeared above the heavenly sky. I saw the vanished dragon. I saw him flying no more. I looked forward. I bowed my head downwards. I smacked my white horse. I smacked my royal horse. I saw my royal horse. I saw my horse running. I saw my horse running forward. I saw my horse running faster. I saw my horse running faster and faster. I rode on my royal horse. I rode on my running horse. I rode forward. I rode faster. I rode faster and faster. I rode faster than a warrior. I rode faster than a soldier. I kept riding. I kept riding forward. I kept riding and riding. I smacked my white horse. I smacked my royal horse. I smacked my horse again. I saw something. I saw something strange. I saw something mysterious. I saw my royal horse. I saw my white horse. I saw my horse running. I saw my horse speeding. I saw my horse over speeding. I saw my royal horse. I saw my white horse. I saw my horse running. I saw my horse running past windy desert. I saw my horse running on muddy desert. I saw my running horse. I saw my over speeding horse. I saw my horse running forward. I saw my horse running past Algerian camels. I saw my horse running past Algerian warriors. I saw my horse running past Algerian knights. I rode on my white horse. I rode on my royal horse. I rode faster. I rode faster and faster. I rode like a royal warrior. I rode like a royal soldier. I rode forward. I rode farther. I rode farther and farther. I approached someone. I approached my heavenly lion. I approached my lion friend. I approached Leo. I saw my white horse. I saw my royal horse. I saw my horse running no more. I saw me and my horse. I saw me and my horse in front of the heavenly lion. I looked forward. I saw my lion friend. I saw him welcoming me to Algeria. I saw my heavenly lion. I saw him welcoming the war veteran and his dragon to Algeria. I saw the heavenly lion. I saw him speaking. I saw him speaking about my journey. I saw him speaking about my travelling. I saw him speaking about the war veteran and his dragon. I saw him speaking about their travelling. I saw the heavenly lion. I saw him congratulating me. I saw him congratulating me for travelling farther. I saw the heavenly lion. I saw him congratulating the war veteran and his dragon. I saw him congratulating them for travelling farther. I saw my lion friend. I saw him praying. I heard him praying. I heard him praying about my journey. I saw him praying about my journey. I saw the heavenly lion. I saw my heavenly friend. I saw him praying. I saw him praying for me. I saw him praying for me and my royal horse. I saw him praying. I heard him praying. I heard him praying for the war veteran and his dragon. I saw my heavenly lion. I saw him walking. I saw him walking behind me. I saw him speaking. I heard him speaking. I saw him mentioning the Lord's Prayer. I heard him mentioning the Lord's Prayer. I looked behind me. I saw my heavenly lion. I saw my lion friend. I saw Leo. I saw him behind me. I saw him blessing me. I saw him blessing the war veteran and his dragon. I looked at the heavenly lion. I looked at my lion friend. I looked at Leo. I saw something. I saw something strange. I saw something. I saw something mysterious. I saw something. I saw something magical. I saw something. I saw something miraculous. I saw something. I saw something heavenly. I saw something. I saw something happening. I saw something. I saw something strange happening. I saw the heavenly lion. I saw my lion friend. I saw Leo. I saw him vanishing. I saw him disappearing. I saw his existence no more. I saw his appearance no more. I looked forward. I bowed my head downwards. I smacked my royal horse. I smacked my white horse. I smacked my running horse the third time. I saw something. I saw something happening. I saw my royal horse. I saw my white horse. I saw my horse running. I saw my horse running faster. I saw my horse running forward. I saw my running horse. I saw my horse running on dirt desert. I saw my horse running on windy desert. I saw my horse running on blowing wind. I rode on my white horse. I rode forward. I rode faster. I rode faster and faster. I rode faster than an Algerian cowboy. I rode faster than an Algerian sailor. I rode faster like an Algerian soldier. I rode faster like a desert soldier. I rode faster. I rode faster and faster. I kept my head downwards. I rode with my head downwards. I rode past Algerian rivers. I rode past Algerian camels. I rode past Algerian mountains. I rode past Algerian cowboys. I rode farther. I rode farther and farther. I rode farther like a royal soldier. I rode farther like a royal warrior. I rode farther like a royal cowboy. I approached somewhere. I approached another nation. I approached another Arab nation. I approached another African nation. I approached another Northern African nation.

CHAPTER 15

Prince Harry and His Journey From Algeria to Morocco

I approached another northern African nation. I approached Morocco. I rode on my white horse. I rode on my royal horse. I rode forward. I rode on another desert. I rode on a Moroccan desert. I rode with my head downwards. I rode faster. I rode faster and faster. I rode on windy desert. I rode like a royal warrior. I rode on dusty desert. I rode on muddy desert. I rode on the desert of Morocco. I felt something. I felt something strange. I felt something mysterious. I felt the warrior wind. I felt the windy desert. I felt the blowing wind. I felt the blowing desert. I felt the dusty desert. I felt warmer. I felt the hot desert. I felt stronger. I felt like a royal cowboy. I felt magnetic. I felt energetic. I felt like a great rider. I felt like a great warrior. I felt magnificent. I felt extremely strong. I felt very happy. I enjoyed the blowing wind. I enjoyed the blowing dirt. I enjoy my riding. I enjoyed my Moroccan journey. I enjoyed riding faster. I enjoyed riding like a warrior. I rode faster. I rode faster and faster. I rode like a royal soldier. I rode like a royal warrior. I rode like a royal stranger. I rode like a royal prince. I rode on muddy desert. I rode on blowing wind. I rode on windy desert. I rode forward. I approached somewhere. I approached someone. I approached another desert. I approached another windy desert. I approached another Moroccan desert. I rode on another dusty desert. I approached someone. I approached another old man. I approached an Arabian old man. I approached a Moroccan old man. I saw him sitting on his camel. I saw him riding on his brown camel. I saw him riding on his brown camel. I saw him wearing a black hoodie. I saw him wearing a black tracksuit. I saw him wearing a cowboy hat. I saw him in front of me. I saw my royal horse. I saw my horse running no more. I saw my horse in front of the old man. I looked forward. I saw the old man. I saw him looking at me. I saw him welcoming me. I saw him welcoming me to Morocco. I saw the old man. I saw him looking at the war veteran and his dragon. I saw him welcoming them to Morocco. I looked at the Arabian old man. I looked at the Moroccan old man. I saw him looking at me. I saw him asking me a question. I saw him asking for my name. I replied him I was from a royal family. I replied him I was Prince Harry. I replied him I was a prince from England. I replied him I was a royal soldier. I replied him I was a royal soldier. I looked at the old man. I looked at the Moroccan old man. I saw him asking me another question. I saw him asking me about my travelling. I saw him asking me about my journey. I looked at the old man. I looked at the Arabian old man. I replied him I was travelling somewhere. I replied him I was travelling towards two warring nations. I replied him I was travelling for peace, unity and freedom. I replied him I was on my journey to a beautiful Island. I replied him I was travelling to Cocos Keeling Islands. I replied him I was travelling in order to bring peace, unity and freedom for two warring nations. I looked at the old man. I looked at the Arabian old man. I looked at the Moroccan old man. I asked him something. I asked him a question. I asked him for his name. I looked at the old man. I saw him replying me. He replied me his name was Dr Morris. I saw Doctor Morris. I saw him smiling. I saw him reaching for his hands. I saw him putting his hands inside his tracksuit. I saw him pulling out armsthing. I saw him pulling out something strange. I saw him pulling out something special. I saw the Moroccan old man. I saw him holding something. I saw him holding a golden stone. I saw Dr Morris. I saw the old man. I saw him holding a round golden stone. I saw him reaching his hands forward. I saw him delivering me the golden stone. I looked at Dr Morris. I reached my hands forward. I grabbed his golden stone. I was holding his golden stone. I held his golden stone. I looked at his golden stone. I admired his golden stone. I felt magnetic. I felt stronger. I felt heavier. I felt magnificent. Felt warmer. I felt like a warrior. I felt like a warrior rider. I felt like a victorious soldier. I felt like a royal soldier. I felt more intelligent. I saw something. I saw something strange. I saw something happening. I saw something strange happening. I saw something. I saw something mysterious. I saw something mysterious happening. I looked at the golden stone. I saw something. I saw something happening. I saw a video of a battle. I saw a video of two warring nations. I saw warring nations. I saw a battle. I saw a battle between two nations. I saw a battle between Sri Lanka and Australia. I saw dead Sri Lankan soldiers. I saw dead Sri Lankan children. I saw dead Sri Lankan women. I saw thousands of dead Sri Lankan soldiers. I saw dead Australian soldiers. I saw dead Australian women. I saw dead Australian children. I saw thousands of dead Australian soldiers. I saw thousands of orphans. I saw thousands of collapsed buildings. I saw thousands of damaged buildings. I saw something. I saw something happening. I saw videos of the battle no more. I saw videos of the war no more. I looked at the golden stone. I saw something. I saw something happening. I saw something. I saw something strange. I saw something strange happening. I saw something. I saw something mysterious. I saw something mysterious happening. I saw my hands shaking. I saw the golden stone. I saw the golden stone shaking. I looked at Dr Morris. I saw him smiling. I looked at the old man. I looked at the Moroccan old man. I looked at the Moroccan old cowboy. I saw him smiling. I smiled with the old man. I saw the old man. I saw him saluting me. I saw him respecting me. I saw him praying for me. I saw him wishing me good luck. I saw the old Moroccan cowboy. I saw him looking at the war veteran and his dragon. I saw the old man. I saw him saluting the war veteran and his dragon. I saw him respecting the war veteran and his dragon. I saw the war veteran and his dragon. I saw their head downwards. I saw them saluting the old man. I saw them respecting the old cowboy. I looked at the old man. I saw him waving goodbye. I saw him waving me goodbye. I saw him waving the war veteran and his dragon goodbye. I looked at the old man of the war. I saw him waving me goodbye. I looked at the old Moroccan man. I smiled with the old man. I waved him goodbye. I saw the old man. I saw him riding on his camel. I saw him riding forward. I looked forward. I looked at the golden stone. I admired the golden stone. I reached my hand downwards. I placed the golden stone inside my pocket. I looked forward. I smacked my royal horse. I smacked my white horse. I smacked my horse for the third time. I saw something. I saw something happening. I saw my royal horse. I saw my white horse. I saw my running horse. I saw my horse running. I saw my horse running faster. I rode on my running horse. I rode with my head downwards. I rode like a warrior. I rode like a royal warrior. I rode like a soldier. I rode like a royal soldier. I rode forward. I rode faster. I rode faster and faster. I rode faster than a warrior. I felt the hot weather. I felt the hot wind. I felt the blowing wind. I felt the moving desert. I felt the dusty wind. I felt the dirty desert. I felt the windy weather. I felt the blowing desert. I kept riding. I kept riding forward. I kept riding farther. I kept riding farther and farther. I rode past warriors. I rode past old warriors. I rode past cowboys. I rode past old cowboys. I rode past Moroccan rivers. I rode past Moroccan mountains. I rode past soldiers. I rode past Moroccan soldiers. I rode past old soldiers. I rode past old veterans. I rode past Moroccan veterans. I rode faster. I rode faster and faster. I rode like a royal warrior. I rode like a royal soldier. I rode like a royal prince. I rode like the prince of England. I rode like a famous prince. I rode faster. I rode faster and faster. I rode faster than a warrior. I rode faster than a royal warrior. I rode faster than a pirate boat. I rode faster than a rollercoaster. I rode faster than a merchant warrior. I rode faster than a pirate warrior. I rode faster. I kept riding. I kept riding farther. I rode farther and farther. I rode farther like a warrior. I rode farther like a royal warrior. I rode farther like a soldier. I rode farther like a royal soldier. I approached somewhere. I approached somewhere beautiful. I approached another Arab nation. I approached another desert nation. I approached another northern African nation.

CHAPTER 16

Prince Harry and His Journey From Morocco to Libya

I approached another North African country. I approached Libya. I rode on my royal horse. I rode on another desert island. I rode on another windy desert. I rode on another muddy desert. I felt the blowing wind. I felt the hot weather. I felt the blowing muds. I felt the crispy warm weather. I felt the blowing hot wind. I felt cold no more. I felt hotter. I felt hotter like a warrior. I felt hotter like a soldier. I felt hotter like a pirate traveller. I felt hotter than a warrior. I felt hotter than a soldier. I felt hotter than a merchant sailor. I felt hotter like a pirate rider. I felt warmer. I felt the warm wind. I rode on my white horse. I rode on my royal horse. I rode on my running horse. I rode with my head downwards. I rode forward. I rode faster. I rode faster and faster. I rode faster like a warrior. I rode faster like a royal warrior. I rode faster. I rode faster and faster. I rode faster like a soldier. I rode faster like a royal soldier. I rode faster. I rode faster and faster. I rode faster and faster. I rode faster like a prince. I rode faster like a royal prince. I rode farther. I rode farther and farther. I kept riding. I kept riding forward. I kept riding. I kept riding forward and forward. I kept riding. I kept riding farther. I kept riding farther and farther. I kept riding. I kept riding forward. I kept riding. I kept riding forward and forward. I kept riding. I kept riding farther. I kept riding farther and farther. I rode on Libyan Desert. I rode past Libyan rivers. I rode past Libyan cowboys. I rode past Libyan mountains. I rode inside Libyan tunnels. I rode inside Libyan tombs. I rode past Libyan women. I rode past Libyan men. I rode past Libyan camels. I rode past Libyan veterans. I rode past Libyan soldiers. I rode past Libyan warriors. I rode on my white horse. I rode on my royal horse. I rode on my running horse. I rode with my head downwards. I rode faster. I rode faster and faster. I rode faster and faster. I rode faster like a pirate warrior. I rode faster like a pirate soldier. I rode faster like a royal warrior. I rode faster like a royal soldier. I rode forward. I rode forward and forward. I kept riding. I kept riding forward. I rode faster. I rode faster and faster. I rode faster. I kept riding. I continued riding faster. I rode farther. I rode farther and farther. I kept riding. I kept riding farther. I kept riding. I kept riding farther and farther. I approached somewhere. I approached a beautiful tomb. I approached a mysterious tomb. I approached a dangerous tomb. I approached a magical tomb. I approached another desert tomb. I approached a Libyan tomb. I approached a tomb of darkness. I rode inside the tomb. I rode inside the tomb of darkness. I rode inside the Libyan tomb. I rode inside the mysterious tomb. I rode faster. I rode faster and faster. I rode faster inside the Libyan tomb. I rode faster inside the tomb of darkness. I kept riding. I kept riding forward. I kept riding inside the mysterious tomb. I kept riding inside the Libyan tomb. I kept riding inside the magical tomb. I approached someone. I approached another friend. I approached a giant dragon. I approached the giant dragon. I saw the giant dragon. I saw the dragon inside the mysterious tomb. I saw the dragon inside the tunnel tomb. I saw the giant dragon. I saw the dragon in front of me. I saw the dragon in front of me, the war veteran and his dragon. I saw my royal horse. I saw my horse running no more. I saw my horse in front of the giant dragon. I saw the war veteran and his dragon. I saw them in front of the giant dragon. I saw the giant dragon. I saw the magical dragon. I saw him doing something. I saw him doing something magical. I saw the giant dragon. I saw him opening his giant mouth. I saw him blowing something. I saw him blowing something magical. I saw him blowing something miraculous. I saw the giant dragon. I saw him blowing a magical fire. I saw him blowing a mysterious fire. I saw him blowing a miraculous fire. I saw him blowing a hot fire. I saw the giant dragon. I saw him speaking. I saw him speaking to me. I saw him speaking to me, the war veteran and his dragon. I saw the giant dragon. I saw him welcoming me. I saw him welcoming me to Libya. I saw the giant dragon. I saw the miraculous dragon. I saw him welcoming the war veteran and his dragon. I saw the giant dragon. I saw him welcoming them to Libya. I saw the giant dragon. I saw the magical dragon. I saw him speaking. I saw him speaking to me. I saw him speaking to me about my journey. I saw him congratulating me. I saw him congratulating me for travelling farther. I saw the giant dragon. I saw the mysterious dragon. I saw him speaking. I saw him speaking to the war veteran and his dragon. I saw the giant dragon. I saw him speaking to them about their journey. I saw the giant dragon. I saw him congratulating the war veteran and his dragon. I saw the giant dragon. I saw him congratulating them for travelling farther. I was inside the Libyan tomb. I was inside the desert tomb. I was inside the tunnel tomb. I was inside the tomb of darkness. I was inside the tunnel of darkness. I was in front of the giant dragon. I was sitting on my royal horse. I looked at the giant dragon. I looked at the magical dragon. I did something. I did something special. I did something royal. I did something respectful. I bowed my head downwards. I saluted the giant dragon. I saw shadows of the war veteran. I saw the war veteran and his dragon. I saw them behind me. I saw the war veteran. I saw him sitting on his dragon. I saw him doing something. I saw the war veteran. I saw him doing something special. I saw the war veteran. I saw him doing something respectful. I saw the war veteran. I saw shadows of the war veteran. I saw the war veteran. I saw him saluting the giant dragon. I saw the war veteran. I saw him respecting the giant dragon. I looked forward. I looked at the giant dragon. I looked at the magical dragon. I looked at the mysterious dragon. I saw the giant dragon. I saw his head downwards. I saw the giant dragon. I saw him respecting me. I saw the giant dragon. I saw him saluting me. I saw the giant dragon. I saw him saluting the war veteran and his dragon. I saw the giant dragon. I saw him respecting the war veteran and his dragon. I saw the giant dragon. I saw him speaking. I saw the giant dragon. I saw him talking. I heard the giant dragon. I heard him talking. I heard him talking about my journey. I saw the giant dragon. I saw him praying for me. I saw the giant dragon. I saw him praying for the war veteran and his dragon. I saw the giant dragon. I saw the giant dragon. I saw the magical dragon. I saw him mentioning the Lord's Prayer. I saw the giant dragon. I saw him speaking. I saw the giant dragon. I saw him speaking about my journey. I saw the giant dragon. I saw him wishing me good luck. I saw the giant dragon. I saw him speaking to the war veteran and his dragon. I saw the giant dragon. I saw him speaking to them about their journey. I saw the giant dragon. I saw him wishing the war veteran and his dragon good luck. I saw the magical dragon. I saw him wishing me good luck. I saw the giant dragon. I saw him speaking to me. I saw the giant dragon. I saw him waving me goodbye. I saw the giant dragon. I saw him speaking. I saw the strange dragon. I saw him speaking to the war veteran and his dragon. I saw the mysterious dragon. I saw him waving them goodbye. I saw the magical dragon. I saw him waving the war veteran and his dragon goodbye. I saw my dragon friend. I saw the giant dragon. I saw him doing something. I saw the giant dragon. I saw him doing something miraculous. I saw the magical dragon. I saw him doing something magical. I saw the giant dragon. I saw him doing something mysterious. I saw the strange dragon. I saw him doing something strange. I saw the mysterious dragon. I saw him doing something mysterious. I saw the giant dragon. I saw him flapping his mighty wings. I saw the magical dragon. I saw him upwards. I saw the heavenly dragon. I saw him flying above the strange tomb. I saw the heavenly dragon. I saw him flying above the tomb of darkness. I saw the giant dragon. I saw him doing something. I saw the giant dragon. I saw him flying. I saw the giant dragon. I saw him flying forward. I saw the giant dragon. I saw something. I saw something mysterious. I saw something. I saw something happening. I saw something. I saw something mysterious happening. I saw something. I saw something strange. I saw something. I saw something strange happening. I saw something. I saw something miraculous. I saw something. I saw something miraculous happening. I saw something. I saw something magical. I saw something. I saw something magical happening. I saw something. I saw the giant dragon. I saw the strange dragon. I saw my dragon friend. I saw something. I saw something happening. I saw the giant dragon. I saw the strange dragon. I saw my dragon friend. I saw him escaping. I saw him vanishing. I saw him disappearing. I saw him escaping the tomb of darkness. I saw the giant dragon no more. I saw my dragon friend no more. I saw the strange dragon no more. I saw the magical dragon no more. I saw he mysterious dragon no more. I looked forward. I smacked my white horse. I smacked my royal horse. I smacked my horse the third time. I saw something. I saw something happening. I saw my royal horse. I saw my white horse. I saw my horse running. I saw my horse running inside the tomb of darkness. I saw my horse running inside the tomb of Libya. I rode on my royal horse. I rode on my white horse. I rode inside the tunnel tomb. I rode inside the strange tomb. I rode inside the mysterious tomb. I rode inside the tunnel tomb. I rode inside the tomb of Libya. I rode forward. I rode faster. I rode faster and faster. I rode faster than a warrior. I rode faster like a warrior. I rode farther. I rode farther and farther. I rode outside the strange tomb. I rode outside the desert tomb. I rode outside the tunnel tomb. I rode outside the tomb of darkness. I rode forward. I rode faster. I rode faster and faster. I rode faster like a royal warrior. I rode faster like a royal soldier. I rode on Libyan Desert. I rode on muddy desert. I rode on hot desert. I rode on windy desert. I felt the blowing hot wind. I felt the crispy weather. I felt cold no more. I felt hotter than a warrior. I felt hotter than a royal warrior. I felt hotter than a soldier. I felt hotter than a royal soldier. I felt the crispy desert weather. I rode on muddy desert. I rode faster. I rode faster and faster. I rode faster than a warrior. I rode faster than a royal warrior. I rode faster than a soldier. I rode faster than a royal soldier. I rode faster. I rode faster and faster. I rode forward. I rode forward and forward. I kept riding. I kept riding forward. I kept riding. I kept riding like a warrior. I kept riding like a royal warrior. I kept riding. I kept riding forward. I kept riding forward. I kept riding. I kept riding forward. I looked forward. I saw the war veteran and his dragon. I saw them flying. I saw them flying above the North African desert. I saw them flying above the hot desert. I saw them flying above the Libyan Desert. I saw them flying. I saw them flying forward. I saw them protecting me. I saw them following me. I saw them ahead of me. I saw the war veteran. I saw him riding. I saw him riding on his heavenly dragon. I saw him following me. I saw him following me and my horse. I looked forward. I rode on my royal horse. I rode with my head downwards. I rode faster. I rode faster and faster. I rode faster like a royal rider. I kept riding like a royal soldier. I rode faster. I rode faster and faster. I kept riding. I kept riding forward. I rode farther. I rode farther and farther. I approached someone. I approached my lion friend. I approached my lion protector. I approached the lion of Judah. I approached my heavenly lion. I approached Leo. I saw my lion friend. I saw him in front of me. I saw him speaking. I saw him welcoming me to Libya. I saw him welcoming the war veteran and his dragon. I saw him welcoming them to Libya. I saw my lion friend. I saw Leo. I saw him speaking. I saw him speaking about my journey. I saw my heavenly lion. I saw my lion friend. I saw him congratulating me. I saw him congratulating me for travelling farther. I saw my lion friend. I saw him speaking. I saw him speaking to the war veteran and his dragon. I saw my lion friend. I saw him speaking about their journey. I saw my heavenly lion. I saw him congratulating the war veteran and his dragon. I saw my lion friend. I saw the lion of Judah. I saw my lion protector. I saw Leo. I saw him congratulating them for travelling farther. I looked forward. I saw my lion friend. I saw him speaking. I saw him speaking to me. I saw him speaking to the war veteran and his dragon. I saw him praying. I saw him praying for me. I saw him praying for the war veteran and his dragon. I saw him mentioning the Lord's Prayer. I saw my lion friend. I saw him speaking. I saw him speaking to me. I saw him speaking about my journey. I saw my heavenly lion. I saw him wishing me good luck. I saw my lion friend. I saw him speaking to the war veteran and his dragon. I saw him speaking to them about their journey. I saw my lion friend. I saw him wishing them good luck. I looked at my lion friend. I saw him speaking. I saw him speaking to me. I saw my lion friend. I saw him waving me goodbye. I looked forward. I looked at my lion friend. I saw my lion friend. I saw him looking forward. I saw him looking at the war veteran and his dragon. I saw my lion friend. I saw my heavenly lion. I saw him speaking. I saw him speaking to the war veteran and his dragon. I saw my lion friend. I saw him waving them goodbye. I looked at my lion friend. I saw my head downwards. I saluted my lion friend. I saw shadows of the war veteran. I saw the war veteran. I saw him sitting on his dragon. I saw his head downwards. I saw him saluting my lion friend. I saw him saluting Leo. I looked forward. I looked at my lion friend. I saw something. I saw something strange. I saw something I saw something strange happening. I saw my heavenly lion. I saw my lion protector. I saw my lion friend. I saw the lion of Judah. I saw Leo. I saw him vanishing. I saw him disappearing. I saw his existence no more. I saw his appearance no more. I looked forward. I smacked my royal horse. I smacked my white horse. I smacked my horse the third time. I saw something. I saw something happening. I saw my royal horse. I saw my white horse. I saw my horse running. I saw my horse running forward. I saw my horse running faster. I saw my horse running faster like a warrior. I saw my running horse. I saw my horse running like a royal rider. I rode on my running horse. I rode with my head downwards. I rode forward. I rode faster. I rode faster and faster. I rode on Libyan Desert. I rode on hot Libyan Desert. I rode on muddy Desert. I felt the blowing wind. I felt the hot windy weather. I felt the blowing hot wind. I rode hotter. I rode like a hot warrior. I rode like a hot soldier. I rode past Libyan Desert. I rode past Libyan rivers. I rode past Libyan mountains. I rode farther. I rode farther and farther. I approached another nation.

CHAPTER 17

Prince Harry and His Journey From Libya to Kenya

I rode farther and farther. I approached another nation. I approached another African nation. I approached another beautiful nation. I approached another beautiful African nation. I approached an eastern African nation. I approached Kenya. I rode on my royal horse. I rode on my white horse. I rode with my head downwards. I rode past Kenyan mountains. I rode past Kenyan castles. I rode past Kenyan tombs. I rode past Kenyan tunnels. I rode past strange tunnels. I rode inside strange Kenyan tombs. I rode inside strange Kenyan tunnels. I rode past Kenyan rivers. I rode past Kenyan mysterious rivers. I looked forward. I saw my heavenly followers. I saw the war veteran and his dragon. I saw them flying. I saw them flying forward. I saw them flying above the Kenyan sky. I saw them flying above the heavenly sky. I saw them flying above the heavenly mountains. I saw them flying above the Kenyan mountains. I saw them flying past Kenyan mountains. I saw them flying above Kenyan tunnels. I saw them flying past Kenyan tunnels. I saw them flying above Kenyan tombs. I saw them flying past Kenyan tombs. I saw them flying forward. I saw them flying above me. I saw them flying in front of me. I smacked my white horse. I smacked my royal horse. I smacked my running horse. I smacked my running horse the last time. I saw something. I saw something happening. I saw my royal horse. I saw my white horse. I saw my horse running. I saw my horse running faster. I saw my horse running faster and faster. I saw my horse running faster like a warrior horse. I saw my horse. I saw my running horse. I saw my horse running. I saw my horse running forward. I saw my white horse. I saw my royal horse. I saw my sprinting horse. I saw my running horse. I saw my horse approaching somewhere. I saw my horse approaching another world. I saw my horse approaching another Kenyan world. I saw my horse approaching a beautiful Kenyan world. I saw my running horse. I saw my horse approaching a Kenyan safari park. I saw my running horse. I saw my white horse. I saw my horse inside Kenyan safari park. I saw my horse running. I saw my running horse. I saw my horse running past Safari Mountains. I saw my running horse. I saw my royal horse. I saw my white horse. I rode on my running horse. I rode on my white horse. I rode on my royal horse. I rode with my head downwards. I rode like a warrior. I rode like a royal warrior. I rode like a soldier. I rode like a royal soldier. I rode like a royal prince. I rode past Kenyan mountains. I rode past Kenyan rivers. I rode inside Kenyan tombs. I rode past Kenyan tombs. I rode inside Kenyan tunnels. I rode past Kenyan tunnels. I rode inside Kenyan forest. I smacked my royal horse. I smacked my white horse. I smacked my sprinting horse. I smacked my running horse. I saw something. I saw something happening. I saw my running horse. I saw my sprinting horse. I saw my white horse. I saw my royal horse. I saw my horse running. I saw my horse running forward. I saw my horse running faster. I saw my horse running faster and faster. I saw my horse running inside Kenyan safari forest. I saw my horse running. I saw my horse running forward. I smacked my sprinting horse. I smacked my running horse. I smacked my white horse. I smacked my royal horse. I smacked my warrior horse the last time. I saw something. I saw something strange. I saw something. I saw something mysterious. I saw something. I saw something strange happening. I saw something. I saw something mysterious happening. I saw my royal horse. I saw my white horse. I saw my running horse. I saw my horse running. I saw my horse running faster. I saw my horse running faster and faster. I saw my sprinting horse. I saw my horse sprinting. I saw my horse sprinting forward. I saw my horse sprinting faster. I saw my horse sprinting faster and faster. I rode on my horse. I rode on my royal horse. I rode on my white horse. I rode on my sprinting horse. I rode forward. I rode inside Kenyan forest. I rode inside Kenyan safari forest. I rode faster. I rode faster and faster. I rode inside Kenyan safari woodlands. I rode forward. I rode faster. I rode faster and faster. I rode farther. I rode farther and farther. I approached somewhere. I approached Kenyan woodlands. I approached Kenyan safari woodlands. I saw my white horse. I saw my royal horse. I saw my running horse. I saw my horse running no more. I saw my horse in front of someone. I saw my horse in front of plenty of Apes. I looked forward. I saw plenty of Apes. I saw Apes on top of trees. I saw some Apes drinking water. I saw some Apes eating fruits. I looked above one tree. I saw someone. I saw a mysterious Ape. I saw the Ape on top of a tree. I saw the Ape climbing downwards. I saw the Ape jumping forward. I saw the Ape jumping towards me. I saw the Ape in front of me. I saw the Ape dancing. I saw the Ape dancing in front of me. I looked forward. I looked at the Ape. I saw the Ape asking me something. I saw the Ape asking me a question. I never understood the Ape. I never understood the Ape's question. I never understood the Ape because it was jumping and speaking. I looked at the Ape. I saw something. I saw the jumping Ape. I saw the mysterious Ape. I saw the writing Ape. I saw the Ape mixing sands and soils with his two hands. I saw the Ape doing something. I saw the Ape writing. I saw the Ape writing something. I saw the Ape writing something with sands and soils. I saw the writing Ape. I saw the Ape showing me signals. I saw the Ape showing me signs. I saw the Ape showing me signs of his writing. I saw the Ape showing his artwork. I saw the Ape showing me his creative artwork. I looked forward. I looked at the Ape. I saw the Ape looking at me. I saw the Ape showing me something. I saw the Ape showing me his name. I looked at the Ape. I looked at his creative artwork. I saw something. I saw the name of the Ape. I saw the word Borun. The Ape was called Borun. I saw Borun. I saw him jumping. I saw him jumping forward. I saw him jumping towards me. I saw Borun. I saw the mysterious Ape. I saw him in front of me. I saw Borun. I saw him asking me a question. I never understood Borun's question. I saw Borun. I saw the mysterious Ape. I saw him jumping forward. I saw him mixing with sands and soils again. I looked at Borun. I saw him looking at me. I saw him speaking. I saw him speaking to me. I heard him speaking about something. I heard him speaking about my name. I looked at Borun. I looked at the mysterious Ape. I spoke to the Ape of the Kenyan woodlands. I spoke to Borun. I explained to Borun about something. I explained to Borun about my name. I told Borun about my name. I told the Ape I was from a royal family. I told the Ape I was a royal prince. I told Borun I was a prince from England. I told Borun I was the prince of England. I saw the Ape of the Kenyan safari woodlands. I saw the Ape inside the Kenyan safari forest. I saw Borun. I saw the mysterious Ape. I saw the talking Ape. I saw the Ape talking. I saw the Ape smiling. I saw the Ape shaking my hands. I saw the Ape talking. I saw the Ape talking to me. I saw the mysterious Ape. I saw the Ape welcoming me. I saw the mysterious Ape. I saw Borun. I saw him looking at the war veteran and his dragon. I saw Borun welcoming them to Kenya. I saw Borun. I saw the Ape of the safari woodlands. I saw the Ape saluting me. I saw the Ape respecting me. I saw the Ape saluting the war veteran and his dragon. I saw the Ape respecting the war veteran and his dragon. I saw the Ape of Kenya. I saw the Ape waving me goodbye. I saw the Ape waving the war veteran and his dragon goodbye. I saw the Ape. I saw Borun. I saw him turning around. I saw him jumping forward. I saw him bouncing forward. I saw him jumping towards something. I saw Borun. I saw him jumping towards his heavenly tree. I saw Borun. I saw the Ape of the safari woodlands. I saw the Ape in front of his heavenly tree. I saw Borun. I saw the Ape climbing his Heavenly tree. I saw Borun. I saw the Ape on top of his heavenly tree. I looked upwards. I saw Borun. I saw my heavenly Ape. I saw my heavenly friend. I saw Borun. I saw him waving me goodbye. I saw shadows of the war veteran and his dragon. I looked upwards. I saw Borun. I saw my Ape friend. I saw him waving the war veteran and his dragon goodbye. I saw Borun. I saw my Ape friend. I saw him waving me goodbye. I reached my hands inside my pocket. I removed something. I removed something special. I removed the Red Booklet. I removed the Book of Freedom. I looked inside the Red Booklet. I saw two warring nations. I saw the war between two blood nations. I saw the battle between Australia and Sri Lanka. I saw fighting Sri Lanka soldiers. I saw fighting Australian soldiers. I saw dead Australian soldiers. I saw dead Sri Lankan soldiers. I saw dead Australian women. I saw dead Sri Lankan women. I saw dead Australian men. I saw dead Sri Lankan men. I saw dead Sri Lankan orphanages. I saw dead Australian children. I saw dead Sri Lankan children. I saw plenty of damaged Sri Lankan buildings. I closed the Red Booklet. I closed the Book of Freedom. I placed the Red Booklet inside my pocket. I looked forward. I smacked my royal horse. I smacked my white horse. I smacked my horse the third time. I saw something. I saw my running horse. I saw my horse running. I saw my horse running forward. I saw my horse running faster. I saw my horse running faster and faster. I rode on my white horse. I rode on my royal horse. I rode forward. I rode inside the Kenyan safari forest. I rode inside the safari woodlands. I rode faster. I rode faster and faster. I rode past Kenyan safari woodlands. I rode outside the Kenyan safari forest. I rode faster. I rode faster and faster. I approached somewhere. I approached the Kenyan safari park. I rode on my royal horse. I rode on my running horse. I rode forward. I rode faster like a warrior. I approached someone. I saw my running horse. I saw my horse running no more. I saw my horse in front of someone. I saw my horse in front of someone special. I saw my horse in front of a heavenly lion. I saw my horse in front of my lion protector. I saw my horse in front of my lion friend. I saw my horse in front of Leo. I was sitting on my horse. I looked forward. I saw Leo. I saw my lion friend. I saw my heavenly lion. I saw him welcoming me. I saw the lion welcoming me to Kenya. I saw shadows of the war veteran and his dragon. I saw my lion friend. I saw him welcoming the war veteran and his dragon. I saw him welcoming them to Kenya. I bowed my head downwards. I saluted my heavenly friend. I saluted my lion friend. I saw shadows of the war veteran and his dragon. I saw the war veteran. I saw him saluting my lion friend. I looked forward. I saw my lion friend. I saw Leo. I saw him speaking. I saw him congratulating me. I saw him congratulating me about my journey. I saw him congratulating me for travelling farther. I saw my lion friend. I saw Leo. I saw him looking at the war veteran and his dragon. I saw my lion friend. I saw Leo. I saw him congratulating the war veteran and his dragon. I saw him congratulating them about their journey. I saw him congratulating them for travelling farther. I saw my lion friend. I saw my heavenly lion. I saw my lion protector. I saw him doing something. I saw him doing something special. I saw him doing something heavenly. I saw my lion friend. I saw my heavenly lion. I saw him praying. I saw him praying for me. I saw him praying for my royal horse. I saw him praying for the war veteran and his dragon. I saw him praying about our journey. I saw him praying about our travelling. I saw my lion friend. I saw him speaking. I saw him saying something. I saw him saying something heavenly. I saw him saying something protective. I saw my lion friend. I saw him mentioning the Lord's Prayer. I looked at my lion friend. I looked at Leo. I saw him waving me goodbye. I saw him waving the war veteran and his dragon goodbye. I looked at my lion friend. I looked at Leo. I saw him doing something. I saw him doing something strange. I saw him doing something mysterious. I saw him doing something miraculous. I saw him doing something magical. I saw him doing something heavenly. I saw my lion friend. I saw him vanishing. I saw him disappearing. I saw his existence no more. I saw his presence no more. I saw his speaking no more. I saw his disappearance. I saw his shadows no more. I looked forward. I smacked my royal horse. I smacked my white horse. I smacked my horse the third time. I saw something. I saw something happening. I saw my royal horse. I saw my white horse. I saw my running horse. I saw my horse running. I saw my horse running forward. I saw my horse running faster. I saw my horse running faster and faster. I saw my horse running past plenty of lions. I saw my horse running past plenty of lionesses. I saw my horse running faster. I saw my horse running faster and faster. I saw my sprinting horse. I saw my running horse. I saw my horse running past the Kenyan safari park. I saw my horse running past Kenyan mountains. I saw my horse running past Kenyan rivers. I saw my horse running past Kenyan warriors. I saw my horse running past Kenyan women. I saw my horse running. I rode on my horse. I rode forward. I rode with my head downwards. I rode faster. I rode faster and faster. I rode like a royal warrior. I rode like a royal soldier. I rode past Kenyan mountains. I rode past Kenyan rivers. I rode past Kenyan warriors. I rode past Kenyan cowboys. I rode faster. I rode faster and farther. I looked forward. I saw shadows of the war veteran and his dragon. I saw the war veteran and his dragon. I saw them flying. I saw them flying above Kenyan mountains. I saw them flying above Kenyan rivers. I saw them flying above the Kenyan safari parks. I saw the war veteran. I saw him sitting on his dragon. I saw him riding on his dragon. I saw him riding forward. I saw him riding faster. I saw him riding above Kenyan mountains. I saw him riding above Kenyan rivers. I saw him riding above Kenyan tombs. I saw him riding above Kenyan tunnels. I saw him flying ahead of me. I rode on my white horse. I rode on my royal horse. I kept riding. I kept riding forward. I kept riding like a warrior. I kept riding like a royal warrior. I kept riding like a soldier. I kept riding like a royal soldier. I continued riding. I continued riding forward. I continued riding like a warrior. I continued riding like a royal warrior. I continued riding like a soldier. I continued riding like a royal soldier. I rode past Kenyan mountains. I rode past Kenyan cowboys. I rode past Kenyan warriors. I rode past Kenyan men. I rode past Kenyan women. I rode past Kenyan rivers. I rode farther. I rode farther and farther. I kept riding farther. I kept riding farther and farther. I approached somewhere. I approached another world. I approached another beautiful world. I approached another nation. I approached another beautiful nation.

CHAPTER 18

Prince Harry and His Journey From Kenya to Ethiopia

I approached another beautiful nation. I approached another African nation. I approached another beautiful African nation. I approached another eastern African nation. I approached Ethiopia. I rode on my horse. I rode on my royal horse. I rode on my white horse. I rode with my head downwards. I rode inside Ethiopian. I rode past Ethiopian mountains. I rode past Ethiopian rivers. I rode past Ethiopian soldiers. I rode past Ethiopian warriors. I rode past Ethiopian men. I rode past Ethiopian women. I rode past Ethiopian rivers. I rode past Ethiopian buildings. I rode past Ethiopian tunnels. I rode past Ethiopian tombs. I rode past Ethiopian mountains. I rode faster. I rode faster and faster. I rode like a warrior. I rode like a royal warrior. I rode like a soldier. I rode like a royal soldier. I rode faster. I rode faster than a warrior. I rode faster than a royal warrior. I rode like a soldier. I rode faster than a soldier. I rode faster than a royal soldier. I kept riding. I kept riding on my running horse. I kept riding forward. I kept riding like a warrior. I kept riding like a royal warrior. I kept riding like a soldier. I kept riding like a royal soldier. I kept riding like a prince. I kept riding like a royal prince. I kept riding faster. I kept riding faster and faster. I looked forward. I looked above me. I looked above the Ethiopian sky. I saw my followers. I saw my flying followers. I saw my heavenly followers. I saw my heavenly protectors. I saw the war veteran and his dragon. I saw them flying above the Ethiopian sky. I saw them following me.

I saw them flying. I looked forward. I looked upwards. I looked above me. I saw the war veteran and his dragon. I saw them following me. I saw them protecting me. I saw them flying. I saw them ahead of me. I saw them flying ahead of me. I looked forward. I rode on my running horse. I rode with my head downwards. I rode forward. I rode forward and forward. I rode faster. I rode faster and faster. I rode farther. I rode farther. I rode farther and farther. I approached a tunnel. I approached an Ethiopian tunnel. I approached a mysterious tunnel. I approached a strange tunnel. I approached a miraculous tunnel. I approached a magical tunnel. I approached a tunnel of darkness. I rode inside the tunnel. I rode inside the Ethiopian tunnel. I rode inside the mysterious tunnel. I rode inside the tunnel of darkness. I rode on my running horse. I rode with my head downwards. I rode forward. I rode forward and faster. I rode faster and faster. I rode faster inside the tunnel of darkness. I rode like a warrior. I rode like a royal warrior. I rode like a soldier. I rode like a royal soldier. I rode inside the Ethiopian tunnel. I rode forward. I rode faster. I rode faster and faster. I approached somewhere. I approached another tunnel. I approached a tomb. I approached a tomb inside the tunnel. I approached a strange tomb. I approached a mysterious tomb. I approached a miraculous tomb. I approached a magical tomb. I approached a holy tomb. I approached a cultural tomb. I approached a deadly tomb. I approached a tomb of darkness. I rode forward. I rode inside the tomb. I rode inside the strange tomb. I rode inside the mysterious tomb. I rode inside the miraculous tomb. I rode inside the magical tomb. I rode inside the cultural tomb. I rode inside the religious tomb. I rode inside the tomb of darkness. I rode forward. I rode forward and forward. I kept riding forward. I continued riding forward. I saw my running horse. I saw my horse running no more. I saw my horse in front of someone. I approached someone. I approached a black man. I approached an Ethiopian black man. I approached a chained black prisoner. I approached a chained black man. I approached a chained Ethiopian prisoner. I looked forward. I saw the black man. I saw the black prisoner. I saw the Ethiopian man. I saw the black Ethiopian man. I saw the black Ethiopian prisoner. I saw the black prisoner. I saw him inside the mysterious tomb. I saw him inside the strange tomb. I saw him inside the magical tomb. I saw something. I saw something strange. I saw something mysterious. I saw the black man. I saw the black Ethiopian prisoner. I saw something. I saw something around him. I saw something strange. I saw something strange around him. I saw something mysterious around him. I saw the black Ethiopian man. I saw the black Ethiopian prisoner. I saw the prisoner of the strange tomb. I saw the prisoner inside the strange tomb. I saw something. I saw something around him. I saw plenty of black chains. I saw plenty of black heavy chains. I saw plenty black strange chains. I saw plenty metallic chains round him. I looked at the black man. I looked at the black prisoner. I looked at the black Ethiopian prisoner. I looked at his hands. I saw plenty of black metallic chains. I saw plenty of black metallic chains around his hands. I saw plenty of black heavy chains. I saw plenty of black heavy chains around his hands. I looked at the black Ethiopian man. I looked at the black Ethiopian prisoner. I looked at the prisoner of the strange tomb. I looked at his legs and feet. I saw something. I saw something strange. I saw something mysterious. I saw something strange around his feet. I saw something mysterious around his feet. I saw something heavy around his feet. I looked at the black man. I looked at the black Ethiopian man. I looked at the black Ethiopian prisoner. I looked at the black prisoner. I looked at the prisoner inside the strange tomb. I saw something. I saw something around his feet. I saw something. I saw something strange. I saw something strange around his feet. I saw something. I saw something heavy. I saw something heavy around his feet. I saw something. I saw something metallic. I saw something. I saw something metallic around his feet. I looked at the black man. I looked at the black Ethiopian man. I looked at the Ethiopian prisoner. I looked at the prisoner inside the strange tomb. I saw him suffering. I saw him overwhelmed. I saw him panicking. I saw him shaking. I saw him shivering. I saw him humming. I saw him breathing like a stranger. I saw him looking at me. I saw him speaking. I saw him speaking to me. I saw him welcoming me. I saw him welcoming me to Ethiopia. I saw him looking at the war veteran and his dragon. I saw the black Ethiopian prisoner. I saw him welcoming the war veteran and his dragon. I looked forward. I looked at the black man. I looked at the black Ethiopian man. I looked at the black prisoner. I saw him speaking. I saw him speaking to me. I saw him saying something. I saw him asking me something. I saw him asking me for something. I saw him asking me for my name. He asked for my name. He asked for my name in a soft tone voice. I heard echoes of his blasted crescendos. I looked at the black prisoner. I looked at the black Ethiopian prisoner. I looked at the black chained man. I looked at the black chained prisoner. I replied him his question. I replied him my name. I replied him I was from a royal family. I replied him I was a royal prince. I replied him I was a prince from England. I replied him I was Prince Harry. I looked forward. I looked at the dying black man. I looked at the dying black prisoner. I looked at the dying black Ethiopian prisoner. I looked at the dying black man inside the strange tomb. I asked him a question. I asked him for his name. He replied me he was a former wizard. He replied me he was a former Ethiopian cowboy. He replied me he was a wizard huntsman. He replied me he used to hunt for people's blood. He replied me he used to hunt for women's blood. He replied me he used to hunt for men's blood. He replied me he used to drink women's blood. He replied me he used to drink men's blood. He replied me he was a wizard. He replied me he was caught by a wizard huntsman. He replied me he was arrested by a wizard huntsman. He replied me he was a prisoner awaiting something. He replied me he was a prisoner awaiting something deadly. He replied me he was a prisoner awaiting something strange. He replied me he was a prisoner awaiting something mysterious. He replied me he was a prisoner awaiting something deadly. He replied me he was a prisoner awaiting his execution. He replied me he was called Peter Johan. I jumped off my white horse. I jumped off my royal horse. I walked forward. I walked towards the black man. I walked towards the black Ethiopian man. I walked towards the black Ethiopian prisoner. I walked towards the black wizard. I walked towards the prisoner inside the strange tomb. I walked towards the chained black prisoner. I walked towards the former wizard. I walked towards the wizard of Ethiopia. I walked towards the prisoner inside the execution chamber. I was in front of the black Ethiopian prisoner. I looked at the black chained man. I looked at his metallic chains. I looked at his heavy chains. I looked at the metallic chains around his hands. I looked at the metallic chains around his feet. I looked at the black man. I looked at the black wizard. I looked at the black dying prisoner. I looked at the wizard inside the strange tomb. I looked at the black prisoner. I looked at the black man. I looked at the black Ethiopian prisoner. I looked at the black Ethiopian wizard. I saw plenty of metallic chains around his hands. I saw plenty of metallic chains around his feet. I saw plenty of heavy chains around his hands. I saw plenty of heavy chains around his feet. I looked at the black prisoner. I saw him looking at me. I wanted to help the black man. I wanted to help him inside the strange tomb. Helping him was harder. I tried my best to remove his heavy chains. I tried my best to remove his metallic chains. I tried my best to help the dying black man. I tried my best to help the dying black prisoner. I tried my best to remove all his chains. I tried my best to remove all his heavy chains. I tried my best to remove all his metallic chains. I tried as hard as I could to help him. I couldn't help him. I couldn't help the dying black man. I couldn't help the dying black wizard. I couldn't help him. I looked at the black Ethiopian man. I looked at the black former wizard. I looked at the black wizard inside his strange tomb. I saw the dying black prisoner. I saw him looking at the prince of England. I saw him looking at Prince Harry. I saw him looking at me. I saw him speaking. I saw him saying something. I saw him speaking to me. I saw him saying something to me. I saw him saying something to me. I saw him praying. I saw him mentioning the Lord's Prayer. I saw something. I saw something happening. I saw something strange. I saw something strange happening. I saw someone. I saw someone appearing. I saw the appearance of someone. I saw the appearance of my heavenly lion. I saw the appearance of my lion friend. I saw the appearance of Leo. I saw Leo. I saw my heavenly lion. I saw my lion friend. I saw him in front of me. I saw him in front of the black man. I saw Leo. I saw my heavenly lion. I saw my Lion friend. I saw him in front of the deadly black man. I saw Leo. I saw my heavenly lion. I saw my lion friend. I saw him speaking. I saw him speaking to the black man. I saw him speaking to the black prisoner. I saw him speaking about his metallic chains. I saw him speaking for his freedom. I saw my heavenly lion. I saw my lion friend. I saw him praying. I saw him praying for the black man. I heard him praying. I heard him praying for the black prisoner. I saw my heavenly lion. I saw my lion friend. I saw Leo. I heard him mentioning the Lord's Prayer. I heard echoes of his blasted crescendos. I looked at the deadly black man. I looked at the deadly black prisoner. I saw something. I saw something strange. I saw something. I saw something happening. I saw something. I saw something strange. I saw something strange happening. I looked at the deadly black man. I looked at the deadly black prisoner. I saw something happening. I saw something strange happening. I saw the disappearance of his chains. I saw the vanishing of all his chains. I saw the disappearance of all the chains around his hands. I saw the disappearance of all the chains around his feet. I saw the freedom of the former wizard. I saw the freedom of the deadly black man. I saw the freedom of the deadly Ethiopian prisoner. I saw the freedom of the dying black man. I saw the freedom of the black prisoner. I saw the freedom of Peter Johan. I looked at Peter Johan. I looked at my deadly prisoner. I saw him running. I saw him running forward. I saw him running faster. I saw him running faster towards me. I saw him hugging me. I saw him hugging his friend. I saw him hugging his royal friend. I saw him hugging me. I grabbed hold of my freed prisoner. I gave him a warmer hug. I saw my freed prisoner. I saw him turning around. I saw him running. I saw him running forward. I saw him running towards his freed friend. I saw him running towards his heavenly lion. I saw him running towards Leo. I saw the deadly black man. I saw the freed black prisoner. I saw him hugging his freed lion. I saw him hugging his heavenly lion. I saw him hugging Leo. I saw my heavenly lion. I saw my freed lion. I saw my lion friend. I saw Leo. I looked at my heavenly lion. I looked at my freed lion. I looked at Leo. I saw something. I saw something happening. I saw something. I saw something strange. I saw something strange happening. I saw my heavenly lion. I saw my freedom. I saw Leo. I saw him vanishing. I saw him disappearing. I saw the vanishing of my heavenly lion. I saw the vanishing of my freed lion. I saw the disappearance of my heavenly lion. I saw the disappearance of my freed lion. I saw the disappearance of my lion friend. I saw the disappearance of Leo. I turned around. I saw my freed friend. I saw my black freed man. I saw my black freed prisoner. I saw him in front of me. I saw him doing something. I saw him holding my hands. I saw him shaking my hands. I saw him respecting me. I saw him praying for me. I saw him praying for the war veteran and his dragon. I saw him praying for me. I saw him praying for my journey. I saw him praying for my followers. I saw him praying for the war veteran and his dragon. I saw him walking towards me. I saw him hugging me. I saw him giving me a hug. I saw him hugging the war veteran and his dragon. I saw the freed black man. I saw the freed black prisoner. I saw him inside his strange tomb. I saw him waving goodbye. I saw him waving me goodbye. I saw him waving my followers goodbye. I saw him waving the war veteran and his dragon goodbye. I looked at the freed black man. I looked at the freed black prisoner. I waved him goodbye. I turned around. I looked at my royal horse. I walked forward. I walked towards my royal horse. I jumped on my royal horse. I sat on my royal horse. I looked forward. I smacked my royal horse. I smacked my white horse. I smacked my horse the third time. I saw something happening. I saw my running horse. I saw my horse running. I saw my horse running forward. I saw my horse running faster. I saw my horse running faster and faster. I saw my running horse. I saw my horse running. I saw my horse outside the strange tunnel. I saw my horse outside the mysterious tomb. I rode on my horse. I rode with my head downwards. I rode forward. I rode faster. I rode faster and faster. I rode past Ethiopian mountains. I rode past Ethiopian rivers. I rode past Ethiopian safari parks. I rode past Ethiopian warriors. I looked forward. I saw the war veteran and his dragon. I saw my heavenly followers. I saw them flying. I saw them flying above the Ethiopian mountains. I saw them ahead of me. I saw them flying ahead of me. I smacked my running horse. I smacked my running horse again. I smacked my running horse the third time. I saw something. I saw something happening. I saw something. I saw something strange. I saw something strange happening. I saw my running horse. I saw my speeding horse. I saw my horse speeding. I saw my horse over speeding. I saw my horse running faster. I saw my horse running faster and faster. I saw my speeding horse. I saw my over speeding horse. I saw my horse approaching somewhere. I saw my horse approaching another world. I approached another nation. I approached another East African nation. I approached Uganda.

CHAPTER 19

Prince Harry and His Journey From Ethiopia to Uganda

I approached Uganda. I approached an African nation. I approached another beautiful nation. I approached another eastern African nation. I approached Uganda. I rode inside Uganda. I rode on my royal horse. I rode on my white horse. I rode on my running horse. I rode with my head downwards. I rode forward. I rode past Ugandan Mountains. I rode past Ugandan rivers. I rode past Ugandan forests. I rode past Ugandan people. I rode past Ugandan men. I rode past Ugandan women. I rode past Ugandan warriors. I rode past Ugandan soldiers. I rode past many Ugandan cows. I rode past many Ugandan horses. I rode past many Ugandan buildings. I rode past many Ugandan heavenly mountains. I rode past many Ugandan rivers. I rode past many Ugandan tunnels. I rode past many Ugandan tombs. I rode past many Ugandan villages. I rode past many Ugandan towns. I rode past many Ugandan cities. I rode past many Ugandan forests. I rode forward. I rode faster. I rode faster and faster. I rode like a warrior. I rode like a royal warrior. I rode like a soldier. I rode like a royal soldier. I approached somewhere. I approached somewhere beautiful. I approached a Ugandan safari park. I rode inside the Ugandan safari park. I rode on my white horse. I rode on my royal horse. I rode on my running horse. I rode inside the safari park. I rode inside the Ugandan safari park. I rode forward. I rode faster. I rode faster and faster. I rode past plenty of Ugandan lions. I rode past plenty of Ugandan lionesses. I saw plenty of Ugandan lions. I saw plenty of Ugandan lionesses. I rode past plenty of Ugandan warriors. I saw plenty of Ugandan warriors. I rode past plenty of Ugandan soldiers. I saw plenty of Ugandan soldiers. I rode past plenty of Ugandan women. I saw plenty of Ugandan women. I rode past plenty of Ugandan men. I saw plenty of Ugandan men. I rode inside the Ugandan safari park. I approached somewhere. I approached somewhere strange. I approached somewhere mysterious. I approached somewhere magical. I approached somewhere miraculous. I approached somewhere full of lions. I approached somewhere full of lioness. I rode forward. I rode faster. I rode faster towards the lions. I rode faster towards the lionesses. I rode faster. I rode faster and faster. I rode faster towards someone. I rode faster towards someone heavenly. I rode faster towards someone protective. I rode faster towards my heavenly lion. I rode faster towards my lion friend. I rode faster towards Leo. I saw the shadows of my horse. I saw my royal horse. I saw my white horse. I saw my running horse. I saw my horse running no more. I saw my white horse. I saw my royal horse. I saw the shadows of my horse. I saw my horse in front of my lion friend. I saw my horse in front of my heavenly lion. I saw my heavenly lion. I saw my lion friend. I saw Leo. I saw him in front of me. I saw him in front of my horse. I saw my heavenly lion. I saw my protective lion. I saw my lion friend. I saw Leo. I saw him in front of the war veteran and his dragon. I saw my heavenly lion. I saw my lion friend. I saw him speaking. I saw him speaking to me. I saw him speaking to the war veteran and his dragon. I heard him speaking. I heard him speaking to me. I heard him speaking to the war veteran and his dragon. I saw my heavenly lion. I saw my lion friend. I saw him welcoming me. I saw him welcoming me to Uganda. I heard my heavenly lion. I heard my lion friend. I heard Leo. I heard him welcoming me. I heard him welcoming me to Uganda. I saw my heavenly lion. I saw my lion protector. I saw my lion friend. I saw him speaking. I saw him speaking to the war veteran and his dragon. I saw him welcoming the war veteran and his dragon. I saw him welcoming them to Uganda. I looked forward. I saw plenty lions. I saw plenty lioness. I saw their head downwards. I saw them saluting me. I saw them saluting the war veteran and his dragon. I saw many lions. I saw many lionesses. I saw them inside the Ugandan safari park. I saw them saluting me. I saw them saluting my horse. I saw them respecting me. I saw them respecting the war veteran and his dragon. I looked at my heavenly lion. I looked at my protector. I looked at my heavenly protector. I looked at my lion friend. I saw something. I saw my heavenly lion. I saw my lion friend. I saw Leo. I saw him speaking. I saw him speaking to me. I saw him speaking about something. I saw him speaking about something strange. I saw him speaking about something mysterious. I saw him speaking about my travelling. I heard him speaking about my mysterious journey. I heard him speaking about my strange journey. I heard my heavenly lion. I heard my lion friend. I heard him congratulating me. I heard him congratulating me for something. I heard him congratulating me for travelling farther. I heard him congratulating the war veteran and his dragon. I heard him congratulating them about their travelling. I heard him congratulating them about their journey. I heard him congratulating them for travelling farther. I looked at my heavenly lion. I looked at my lion friend. I looked at Leo. I saw something. I saw something happening. I saw something. I saw something strange. I saw something. I saw something strange happening. I saw something. I saw something mysterious. I saw something I saw something mysterious happening. I looked at my heavenly lion. I looked at my lion friend. I looked at Leo. I saw him vanishing. I saw him disappearing. I saw his vanishing. I saw his disappearance. I saw his appearance no more. I saw his existence no more. I saw his shadows no more. I heard him speaking no more. I looked forward. I reached out my hands. I placed my hands inside my pocket. I removed something. I removed something miraculous. I removed something magical. I removed my Red Booklet. I removed the red Book of Freedom. I opened the Red Booklet. I opened the Book of Freedom. I looked inside the Red Booklet. I looked inside the Book of Freedom. I saw something. I saw something strange. I saw something. I saw something mysterious. I saw something. I saw something magical. I saw something. I saw something miraculous. I saw the battle of two blood nations. I saw the battle of two blood armies. I saw the battle of Australia and Sri Lanka armies. I saw Australian and Sri Lankan soldiers. I saw Australian and Sri Lankan armies. I saw plenty of dead Australian soldiers. I saw plenty of dead Sri Lankan soldiers. I saw plenty of dead Australian women. I saw plenty of dead Sri Lankan women. I saw plenty of dead Australian men. I saw plenty of dead Sri Lankan men. I saw plenty of dead Australian children. I saw plenty of dead Sri Lankan children. I saw plenty of dead Australian orphans. I saw plenty of dead Sri Lankan orphans. I shook my head in disbelief. I couldn't watch the battle anymore. I closed the Red Booklet. I closed the Book of Freedom. I reached my hands downwards. I reached my hands towards my pocket. I placed the Red Booklet inside my royal pocket. I looked forward. I smacked my white horse. I smacked my royal horse. I saw something. I saw something happening. I saw something. I saw something strange. I saw something strange happening. I saw my white horse. I saw my royal horse. I saw my horse running. I saw my horse running forward. I saw my horse running faster. I saw my horse running past plenty of lions. I saw my horse running past plenty of lionesses. I saw my running horse. I saw my speeding horse. I saw my horse running past the Ugandan safari park. I saw my horse running past plenty of Ugandan villages. I saw my horse running past plenty of Ugandan safari parks. I saw my horse running past plenty of Ugandan towns. I saw my horse running past plenty of Ugandan cities. I saw my horse running past plenty of Ugandan mountains. I saw my horse running past plenty of Ugandan rivers. I saw my horse running past plenty of Ugandan forests. I saw my horse running past plenty of Ugandan schools. I saw my horse running past plenty of Ugandan buildings. I saw my horse running past plenty of Ugandan warriors. I saw my horse running past plenty of Ugandan cowboys. I saw my running horse. I saw my horse approaching somewhere. I saw my running horse. I saw my horse approaching another world. I saw my running horse. I saw my horse approaching another beautiful world. I saw my running horse. I saw my horse approaching another beautiful forest. I saw my running horse. I saw my horse running inside a beautiful forest. I rode on my running horse. I rode with my head downwards. I rode forward. I rode faster. I rode faster and faster. I rode inside a beautiful forest. I rode inside a Ugandan forest. I rode inside a raining forest. I rode inside a muddy forest. I rode inside a strange forest. I rode inside a mysterious forest. I rode inside a forest of darkness. I rode faster. I rode faster and faster. I rode past plenty of woodlands. I rode past plenty of strange woodlands. I rode past plenty of mysterious woodlands. I rode past plenty of Apes. I rode past plenty of wild creatures. I rode past African leopards. I rode past Ugandan Leopards. I rode past Ugandan wild creatures. I rode on my running horse. I approached someone. I approached someone strange. I approached someone mysterious. I approached someone dangerous. I approached a giant lion. I saw a giant lion. I saw a dangerous lion. I saw a strange lion. I saw the lion running. I saw the lion running forward. I saw the lion running towards me. I saw the strange lion. I saw the dangerous lion. I saw the lion running. I saw the lion running forward. I saw the giant lion. I saw the lion running. I saw the lion running towards me and my horse. I saw the war veteran and his dragon. I saw the war veteran. I saw his giant dragon. I saw his dragon landing. I saw his dragon landing aggressively. I saw his dragon landing in front of the dangerous lion. I looked at the veteran's dragon. I saw his dragon doing something. I looked at the veteran's dragon. I saw something. I saw something happening. I saw something. I saw something strange. I saw something. I saw something strange happening. I saw something. I saw something mysterious. I saw something. I saw something mysterious happening. I looked forward. I looked at the veteran's dragon. I saw the veteran's dragon. I saw his dragon in front of the dangerous lion. I saw his dragon in front of the strange lion. I saw his dragon in front of the giant lion. I saw his dragon opening his giant mouth. I saw something. I saw something strange. I saw something mysterious. I saw something miraculous. I saw something magical. I saw the veteran's dragon. I saw his dragon blowing out something. I saw his dragon blowing out something strange. I saw his dragon blowing out something mysterious. I saw his dragon blowing out something magical. I saw his dragon blowing out something miraculous. I saw the war veteran and his dragon. I saw his dragon blowing out hot red fire. I looked forward. I looked at the giant lion. I looked at the dangerous lion. I looked at the strange lion. I looked at the aggressive lion. I saw something. I saw something happening. I saw something happening to the giant lion. I saw something. I saw something happening to the strange lion. I saw something. I saw something happening to the dangerous lion. I saw the giant lion. I saw the strange lion. I saw the dangerous lion. I saw the wild lion. I saw the lion defeated. I saw the lion blown away. I saw the lion blown away aggressively. I saw the lion smashed onto a black tree. I saw the lion defeated. I looked at the dangerous lion. I looked at the giant lion. I looked at the strange lion. I looked at the giant lion. I looked at the finished lion. I looked at the defeated lion. I saw the defeated lion. I saw the defeated giant lion. I saw the breathless giant lion. I saw the giant lion. I saw the dangerous lion. I saw the aggressive lion. I saw the finished giant lion. I saw him not breathing. I saw his breathing no more. I saw his aggression no more. I saw him finished nearby a giant black tree. I saw the lion dead nearby a giant black tree. I saw the giant lion. I saw the stranger lion. I saw the strange lion. I saw him dead. I saw the giant lion. I saw the defeated giant lion. I saw him dead and breathless. I looked at the giant lion. I looked at the strange lion. I looked at the defeated giant lion. I looked at the finished giant lion. I saw something. I saw something happening. I saw something. I saw something strange. I saw something. I saw something strange happening. I saw something. I saw something mysterious. I saw something. I saw something mysterious happening. I saw something. I saw something magical. I saw something. I saw something magical happening. I saw something. I saw something miraculous. I saw something. I saw something miraculous happening. I saw something. I saw something glorious. I saw something. I saw something glorious happening. I saw something. I saw something victorious. I saw something I saw something victorious happening. I saw something. I saw something heavenly. I saw something. I saw something heavenly happening. I saw the giant lion. I saw the defeated lion. I saw the deadly lion. I saw the finished lion. I saw the dangerous lion. I saw the lion vanishing. I saw the lion disappearing. I saw the vanished giant lion. I saw the vanished defeated lion. I saw the vanished dead lion. I saw the vanished deadly lion. I saw the vanished lion. I saw the disappeared lion. I saw the disappearance of the giant lion. I saw the vanishing of the dangerous lion. I saw the dangerous lion. I saw the dangerous lion no more. I saw the giant lion no more. I saw the strange lion no more. I saw the aggressive lion no more. I saw the defeated lion no more. I saw the giant lion's existence no more. I looked forward. I saw the war veteran and his dragon. I saw the victorious dragon. I saw the glorious dragon. I saw my heavenly dragon. I saw my mysterious dragon. I saw my dragon protector. I saw my dragon follower. I saw my dragon rising upwards. I saw my dragon flying upwards. I saw my dragon flying above the raining forest. I saw my dragon flying above the black trees. I saw my dragon flying above the heavenly woodlands. I saw the war veteran and his dragon. I saw them flying. I saw them flying above the raining forest. I saw them flying above the black trees. I saw them flying forward. I saw them flying above the heavenly woodlands. I saw them flying. I saw them flying ahead of me. I saw them following me. I saw them following me and my royal horse. I looked forward. I saw something. I saw my shadows. I saw my black shadows. I bowed downwards. I saw my shadows. I saw my black shadows. I saw my head downwards. I smacked my white horse. I smacked my royal horse. I smacked my horse the third time. I saw something. I saw my white horse. I saw my royal horse. I saw my running horse. I saw my horse running. I saw my horse running forward. I saw my horse running faster. I saw my horse running inside the Ugandan forest. I saw my horse running inside the raining forest. I saw my horse running past Ugandan woodlands. I saw my horse running inside Ugandan woodlands. I saw my horse running past raining woodlands. I saw my horse running past muddy woodlands. I rode on my white horse. I rode on my royal horse. I rode with my head downwards. I rode inside Ugandan raining forest. I rode inside Ugandan raining woodlands. I rode faster. I rode faster and faster. I rode faster like a warrior. I rode faster like a royal warrior. I rode faster like a soldier. I rode faster like a royal soldier. I rode faster. I rode faster and faster. I approached somewhere. I rode outside the Ugandan raining forest. I rode faster. I rode faster and faster. I rode past plenty of Ugandan safari parks. I rode past plenty of Ugandan forest. I rode past plenty of Ugandan villages. I rode past plenty of Ugandan towns. I rode past plenty of Ugandan landscapes. I rode past plenty of Ugandan rivers. I rode past plenty of Ugandan mountains. I rode past plenty of Ugandan cities. I rode past plenty of Ugandan cowboys. I rode past plenty of Ugandan veterans. I rode past plenty of Ugandan warriors. I rode past plenty of Ugandan women. I rode past plenty of Ugandan soldiers. I rode past plenty of Ugandan farmers. I rode with my head downwards. I saw my black shadows. I looked backwards. I saw my heavenly followers. I saw my heavenly protectors. I saw the war veteran and his dragon. I saw them flying above the Ugandan sky. I saw them following me. I saw them following me and my running horse. I looked forward. I rode on my running horse. I rode with my head downwards. I saw my shadows.

I saw my black shadows. I smacked my white horse. I smacked my royal horse. I smacked my horse the third time. I saw something. I saw something happening. I saw something. I saw something strange. I saw something. I saw something strange happening. I saw something. I saw something mysterious. I saw something. I saw something mysterious happening. I saw something. I saw the shadows of someone. I saw the shadows of my running horse. I saw black shadows of my running horse. I saw something. I saw something happening. I saw my running horse. I saw my horse speeding. I saw my horse over speeding. I saw my horse running faster. I saw my horse running faster and faster. I saw my running horse. I saw my horse approaching somewhere. I saw my horse approaching another world. I saw my running horse. I saw my speeding horse. I saw my horse running past all African nations. I saw my running horse. I saw my horse approaching northern America. I saw my running horse. I saw my horse approaching a northern American nation. I saw my running horse. I saw my horse inside northern America. I saw my running horse. I saw my horse running inside a northern American nation.

CHAPTER 20

Prince Harry and His Journey From Uganda to Canada

I saw my running horse. I saw my horse inside a beautiful nation. I saw my speeding horse. I saw my horse inside a northern American nation. I saw my over speeding horse. I saw my horse inside a blood nation. I saw my royal horse. I saw my horse running. I saw my horse approaching a blood nation. I saw my running horse. I saw my horse approaching Canada. I saw my running horse. I saw my royal horse. I saw my white horse. I saw my speeding horse. I saw my over speeding horse. I saw my horse inside a northern American nation. I saw my running horse. I saw my horse inside a bloody nation. I saw my over speeding horse. I saw my horse inside Canada. I saw my running horse. I saw my horse running. I saw my horse running past Canadian mountains. I saw my running horse. I saw my horse running past Canadian snowing mountains. I saw my running horse. I saw my horse running past snowing landscapes. I saw my running horse. I saw my horse running past Canadian cowboys. I saw my running horse. I saw my horse running past Canadian snowing tunnels. I saw my running horse. I saw my horse running past Canadian women. I rode on my running horse. I rode forward. I rode inside a bloody nation. I rode inside a northern American nation. I rode inside Canada. I rode with my head downwards. I rode faster. I rode faster and faster. I rode faster like a warrior. I rode faster like a royal warrior. I rode faster. I rode faster like a soldier. I rode faster. I rode faster like a royal solider. I rode past plenty of mountains. I rode faster. I rode past plenty of Canadian mountains. I rode faster. I rode past landscapes. I rode faster. I rode past plenty of Canadian landscapes. I rode faster. I rode past snowing mountains. I rode faster. I rode past plenty of Canadian snowing mountains. I rode faster. I rode past plenty of Canadian creatures. I rode faster. I rode past plenty of Canadian warriors. I rode faster. I rode past plenty of Canadian soldiers. I rode faster. I rode past plenty of Canadian veterans. I rode faster. I rode past plenty of Canadian merchants. I rode faster. I rode past plenty of Canadian cowboys. I rode faster. I rode past Canadian rivers. I rode faster. I rode past plenty of Canadian rivers. I rode on my royal horse. I rode on my white horse. I rode on my running horse. I rode faster. I rode faster and faster. I rode like a warrior. I rode like a cold warrior. I rode like a snowing warrior. I felt crispy cold. I felt colder and colder. I felt the breezing cold wind. I felt the shivering cold weather. I felt crispy cold in Canada. I felt the crispy cold weather. I turned my head around. I looked backwards. I saw the war veteran and his dragon. I saw my heavenly protectors. I saw my heavenly followers. I saw them flying. I saw them flying above the mountains. I saw them flying above the Canadian mountains. I saw them flying above the snowing mountains. I saw them following me. I saw them following me and my running horse. I turned my head around. I looked forward. I smacked my running horse. I smacked my speeding horse. I smacked my over speeding horse the third time. I saw something. I saw something happening. I saw something. I saw something strange happening. I saw something. I saw something mysterious happening. I saw my running horse. I saw my horse speeding. I saw my horse over speeding. I rode forward. I rode faster. I rode faster and faster. I rode faster than a warrior. I rode faster than a running warrior. I rode faster than a soldier. I rode faster than a running soldier. I rode farther. I rode farther and farther. I rode on my running horse. I rode with my head downwards. I rode farther. I rode farther and farther. I approached somewhere. I approached somewhere beautiful. I approached somewhere heavenly. I approached a strange river. I approached a mysterious river. I approached a massive river. I approached a snowing river. I saw my royal horse. I saw my horse running no more. I saw my horse in front of a massive river. I saw my horse in front of a snowing river. I looked forward. I saw the massive river. I looked inside the river. I saw shadows of someone. I saw shadows of someone friendly. I saw shadows of my warrior horse. I saw shadows of my royal horse. I turned around. I looked backwards. I saw my heavenly protectors. I saw my heavenly followers. I saw the war veteran and his dragon. I saw them flying no more. I saw them standing. I saw them standing behind me. I saw them relaxing. I saw shadows of my white horse. I saw shadows of my royal horse. I jumped off my white horse. I jumped away from my royal horse. I grabbed my white horse. I grabbed my white horse. I reached for my hands. I cleaned all the dirt away from my royal horse. I grabbed the head of my royal horse. I pulled my horse forward. I pulled my horse towards the river. I pulled my royal horse towards the snowing river. I saw my white horse. I saw my royal horse. I saw my horse looking at the river. I looked inside the snowing river. I looked inside the Canadian river. I saw shadows of my royal horse. I stood in front of the river. I stood nearby my horse. I watched my royal horse. I saw something. I saw my royal horse. I saw my white horse. I saw my tired horse. I saw my snowing horse. I saw my horse doing something. I saw my horse drinking. I saw my horse drinking water. I looked inside the snowing river. I saw shadows of my horse. I saw shadows of my drinking horse. I saw my drinking horse. I watched my tired horse. I watched my horse drinking water. I watched my horse. I watched until my horse finished drinking water. I watched my horse wondering. I saw my royal horse. I saw my horse wandering around. I saw my horse wandering around the snowing river. I sat nearby the snowing river. I sat on the snowing ground. I sat and watched my wandering horse. I sat nearby the Canadian river. I relaxed myself. I turned around. I saw my heavenly protectors. I saw my heavenly followers. I saw the war veteran and his dragon. I saw them behind me. I saw them sleeping. I saw them sleeping behind me. I relaxed myself all night. I felt the crispy cold weather. I felt the snowing wind. I felt the blowing wind. I felt colder. I felt sleepier. I fell asleep. I slept all night. I slept feeling the crispy cold weather. I woke up the next morning. I walked forward. I walked towards the snowing river. I washed my handsome face. I jumped inside the river. I looked inside the waters. I saw myself. I saw myself swimming. I saw my shadows. I saw shadows of myself. I saw shadows of myself swimming. I enjoyed swimming. I enjoyed swimming inside the snowing river. I finished swimming inside the snowing river. I jumped away from the snowing river. I looked forward. I saw my heavenly protectors. I saw my heavenly followers. I saw the war veteran and his dragon. I saw them sleeping no more. I saw them in front of me. I saw the war veteran. I saw him sitting on his dragon. I walked forward. I walked towards my royal horse. I jumped onto my royal horse. I sat on my royal horse. I saw something. I saw my royal horse. I saw my horse turning around. I saw my horse facing forward. I turned backwards. I saw the war veteran. I saw him sitting on his dragon. I saw him getting ready for flying. I saw my heavenly protectors. I saw my heavenly followers. I saw them behind me. I turned around. I smacked my white horse. I smacked my royal horse. I smacked my horse the third time. I saw something. I saw something happening. I saw something. I saw something strange. I saw something. I saw something strange happening. I saw my royal horse. I saw my white horse. I saw my horse running. I saw my horse running forward. I rode on my horse. I rode on my royal horse. I rode on my white horse. I rode on my running horse. I saw my running horse. I saw my horse running. I saw my horse running past the river. I saw my horse running past the snowing river. I saw my running horse. I saw my horse leaving the snowing river. I saw my horse running. I saw my horse running forward. I rode on my running horse. I rode with my head downwards. I rode past the snowing river. I rode past Canadian mountains. I rode past snowing mountains. I rode past Canadian cowboys. I rode past Canadian buildings. I rode past Canadian landscapes. I rode past snowing tunnels. I rode past snowing castles. I rode past snowing tombs. I rode faster inside snowing tunnels. I rode faster outside snowing tunnels. I rode faster inside snowing tombs. I rode faster outside snowing tombs. I rode faster and faster. I approached a snowing forest. I approached a Canadian forest. I approached a snowing Canadian forest. I rode inside the Canadian forest. I rode inside the snowing Canadian forest. I rode forward. I rode faster. I rode faster and faster. I rode inside snowing woodlands. I rode past many snowing trees. I rode past many snowing woodlands. I rode faster. I rode faster and faster. I rode faster like a warrior. I rode faster like a royal warrior. I rode faster like a soldier. I rode faster like a royal soldier. I approached somewhere. I approached somewhere inside the snowing forest. I approached somewhere full of woodlands. I approached somewhere full of snowing woodlands. I approached someone. I approached a woman. I approached a white woman. I looked forward. I saw a white woman. I saw a white woman. I saw her sitting on a white horse. I saw her sitting on her horse. I saw her wearing something. I saw her wearing something massive. I saw her wearing a massive white hoodie. I saw her in front of me. I looked forward. I looked at the white woman. I saw her looking at me. I saw her speaking. I saw her welcoming me. I saw her welcoming the war veteran and his dragon. I saw the white woman. I saw her asking me a question. I saw her asking me for my name. I saw her asking for my name and my journey. I saw her asking me where I was travelling towards. I looked at the white woman. I replied her I was from a royal family. I replied her I was from England. I replied her I was a prince from England. I replied her I was Prince Harry. I replied her I was travelling towards somewhere. I replied her I was travelling towards another nation. I replied her I was travelling towards Sri Lanka. I looked at the white woman. I asked her something. I asked her a question. I asked her for her name. I asked her where she was travelling towards. I looked forward. I looked at the white woman. I saw her speaking. I saw her answering my question. She replied me she was the queen of Canada. She replied me she was also a witch. She replied me she was a witch huntswoman. She replied me she was heading towards the woodlands. She replied me she was searching for human blood. She replied me she was searching for human blood. She replied me she was called Witch Amy. I looked at the white woman. I looked at Witch Amy. I saw her putting her hands inside her pocket. I saw her removing something. I saw her removing an empty cup. I saw her looking inside the empty cup. I saw her chanting. I saw her performing witchcraft. I looked at the white woman. I looked at the Canadian witch. I looked at Witch Amy. I saw her looking at me. I saw her holding the magical cup. I saw her reaching out her hands. I saw her reaching her hands forward. I saw her delivering me the magical cup. I look inside the magical cup. I saw icy water inside the magical cup. I looked at the white witch. I looked at Witch Amy. I grabbed her magical cup. I was holding her magical cup. I held her magical cup. I saw the white witch. I saw Witch Amy. I saw her looking at me. I saw her blinking her eyes. I saw her giving me orders. I saw her ordering me to drink her magical icy water. I drank her icy cold water. I drank her magical water. I felt magical. I felt changed. I felt charged. I felt stronger. I felt magnetic. I felt energetic. I felt like a stranger. I felt mysterious. I felt like a royal warrior. I felt like a royal soldier. I looked at the queen of Canada. I looked at Witch Amy. I saw her looking at me. I saw her smiling. I smiled with her. I saw her speaking. I saw Witch Amy. I saw the white woman. I saw the queen of Canada. I saw her praying. I saw her praying for me. I saw her praying for my journey. I saw her praying for the war veteran and his dragon. I saw her praying for their journey. I looked at the white woman. I looked at the magical witch. I looked at the witch of the snowing woodlands. I saw her praying. I saw her mentioning the Lord's Prayer. I looked at the white woman. I looked at the white witch. I looked at the witch of the snowing forest. I thanked her. I thanked her for her helpful behaviour. I gave her thanks. I saw the white woman. I saw the magical witch. I saw her waving me goodbye. I saw her waving the war veteran and his dragon goodbye. I looked at the white witch. I looked at witch Amy. I saw her smacking her white horse. I saw her smacking her white horse again. I saw her smacking her white horse the third time. I saw something. I saw something happening. I saw her white horse. I saw her horse running. I saw her horse running forward. I looked forward. I smacked my white horse. I smacked my royal horse. I saw something. I saw something happening. I saw my white horse. I saw my running horse. I saw my horse running. I saw my horse running forward. I rode on my horse. I rode on my royal horse. I rode on my running horse. I rode with my head downwards. I rode inside the snowing woodlands. I rode forward. I rode faster. I rode faster and faster. I rode past plenty snowing woodlands. I rode past plenty snowing trees. I rode inside the snowing forest. I rode past plenty of snowing rivers. I turned my head around. I turned my head backwards. I saw my heavenly followers. I saw the war veteran and his dragon. I saw them flying above the snowing woodlands. I saw them following me and my running horse. I turned my head around. I looked forward. I rode on my running horse. I rode faster. I rode faster like a warrior. I rode outside the snowing forest. I rode faster. I rode faster and faster. I rode farther. I rode farther away from the snowing forest. I rode past mountains. I rode past snowing mountains. I rode past plenty nations. I rode past plenty North American nations. I rode past plenty American nations. I rode past plenty South American nations. I rode past plenty Central American nations. I rode farther. I rode farther and farther. I rode inside Asian nations. I rode past plenty of Asian nations. I rode past plenty of northern Asian nations. I rode past plenty of eastern Asian nations. I rode past plenty of western Asian nations. I rode faster. I rode farther. I rode farther and farther. I approached somewhere. I approached another nation.

CHAPTER 21

Prince Harry and His Journey From Canada to Sri Lanka

I approached another nation. I approached another beautiful nation. I approached Australia. I rode inside Australia. I rode on my running horse. I rode with my head downwards. I rode forward. I rode faster. I rode faster and faster. I rode faster like a warrior. I rode faster like royal warrior. I rode like a soldier. I rode faster like a royal soldier. I rode past mountains. I rode past Australian mountains. I rode past snowing mountains. I rode past snowing Australian mountains. I rode past Australian rivers. I rode past plenty of Australian rivers. I rode inside an Australian forest. I rode past Australian woodlands. I rode past snowing Australian woodlands. I approached somewhere. I approached another snowing woodlands. I saw my horse running no more. I saw my horse in front of something. I saw my horse in front of plenty of snowing woodlands. I reached out my hands. I placed my hands inside my pocket. I removed something. I removed the Red Booklet. I removed the Book of Freedom. I held the Book of Freedom. I was holding the Book of Freedom. I opened the Red Booklet. I opened the Book of Freedom. I looked inside the Red Booklet. I looked inside the Book of Freedom. I saw something. I saw something happening. I saw something. I saw something strange. I saw something. I saw something strange happening. I saw something. I saw something mysterious. I saw something. I saw something mysterious happening. I saw something. I saw something miraculous. I saw something. I saw something miraculous happening. I saw something. I saw something magical. I saw something. I saw something magical happening. I saw something. I saw something happening. I saw a battle in Sri Lanka. I saw the battle of two bloody nations. I saw the war between two bloody nations. I saw the war between Australia and Sri Lanka. I saw the battle in Sri Lanka. I saw Australia invading Sri Lanka. I saw Australian soldiers fighting in Sri Lanka. I saw many collapsed Sri Lankan buildings. I saw the war in Sri Lanka. I saw Sri Lankan soldiers fighting Australian soldiers. I saw plenty dead Sri Lankan soldiers. I saw plenty dead Australian soldiers. I saw plenty of dead Sri Lankan women. I saw plenty of dead Australian women. I saw plenty of dead Sri Lankan warriors. I saw plenty of dead Australian warriors. I saw plenty of dead Sri Lankan veterans. I saw plenty of dead Australian veterans. I saw plenty of dead Sri Lankan children. I saw plenty of dead Australian children. I saw plenty of dead Sri Lankan armies. I saw plenty of dead Australian armies. I closed the Red Booklet. I closed the Book of Freedom. I shook my head. I shook my head again. I shook my head the third time. I shook my head in disbelief. I reached my hands downwards. I placed the Red Booklet inside my pocket. I looked forward. I smacked my royal horse. I smacked my white horse. I smacked my horse the third time. I saw something. I saw something happening. I saw my running horse. I saw my horse running. I saw my horse running forward. I saw my horse running inside the Australian woodlands. I saw my horse running faster. I saw my horse running past plenty of snowing woodlands. I saw my horse running past plenty of snowing trees. I saw my running horse. I saw my horse running outside the Australian forest. I saw my running horse. I saw my horse running outside the snowing woodlands. I saw my running horse. I saw my horse running. I saw my horse running faster. I saw my horse running faster and faster. I saw my horse running past plenty of Australian forests. I saw my horse running past plenty Australian mountains. I saw my horse running past plenty of Australian rivers.

I saw my horse running faster. I saw my horse running past plenty of Australian tunnels. I saw my running horse. I saw my horse running past plenty of Australian castles. I saw my running horse. I saw my horse running past plenty of Australian royal castles. I saw my running horse. I saw my horse running past plenty of tombs. I saw my running horse. I saw my horse running past plenty of Australian warriors. I saw my running horse. I saw my horse running past plenty of Australian cowboys. I saw my running horse. I saw my horse running past plenty of Australian old buildings. I rode on my running horse. I rode with my head downwards. I rode forward. I rode past plenty of Australian mountains. I rode past plenty of Australian rivers. I rode past plenty of Australian cowboys. I rode past plenty of Australian creatures. I rode past plenty of Australian forests. I rode inside plenty of Australian forests. I rode past plenty of Australian woodlands. I rode faster. I turned my head around. I turned my head backwards. I saw my heavenly followers. I saw the war veteran and his dragon. I saw them flying above the Australian mountains. I saw them flying behind me and my horse. I turned my head around. I looked forward. I saw my head downwards. I looked downwards. I saw my shadows. I smacked my running horse. I smacked my running horse again. I smacked my running horse the third time. I rode faster and faster. I rode faster like a warrior. I rode faster like a royal warrior. I rode like a soldier. I rode faster. I rode faster like a royal soldier. I rode farther. I rode farther and farther. I rode farther like a warrior. I rode farther like a royal warrior. I rode farther. I rode farther and farther. I rode farther like a soldier. I rode farther. I rode farther like a royal soldier. I approached somewhere. I approached somewhere beautiful. I approached another nation. I approached a warring nation. I approached Sri Lanka. I rode inside Sri Lanka. I rode on my running horse. I rode past Sri Lankan landscapes. I rode inside Sri Lankan forests. I rode inside Sri Lankan rain forests. I rode inside Sri Lankan raining woodlands. I past Sri Lankan raining trees. I looked downwards. I saw my shadows. I saw my riding shadows. I saw my horse shadows. I saw my horse not running any more. I saw my horse in front of someone. I saw my horse in front of someone heavenly. I saw my horse in front of my heavenly lion. I saw my horse in front of my lion friend. I saw my horse in front of the lion of Judah. I saw my horse in front of Leo. I looked forward. I saw my heavenly lion. I saw my lion friend. I saw Leo. I saw him speaking. I saw him speaking to me. I saw my heavenly lion. I saw him welcoming me and my horse. I saw my heavenly lion. I saw him welcoming the war veteran and his dragon. I saw my lion friend. I saw him welcoming us to Sri Lanka. I saw my lion protector. I saw him welcoming us to something. I saw him welcoming us about our travelling. I saw him welcoming us about our mysterious journey. I saw him welcoming us for travelling farther. I looked forward. I looked at my lion friend. I looked at my heavenly lion. I looked at Leo. I saw him speaking. I saw him praying. I saw him praying for me and my horse. I saw him praying for my heavenly followers. I saw him praying for the war veteran and his dragon. I saw him mentioning the Lord's Prayer. I looked forward. I looked at my heavenly lion. I saw something. I saw something happening. I saw something. I saw something strange. I saw something. I saw something strange happening. I saw something. I saw something magical. I saw something. I saw something magical happening. I saw something mysterious. I saw something mysterious happening. I saw my heavenly lion. I saw my heavenly protector. I saw my lion friend. I saw Leo. I saw him vanished. I saw him vanishing. I saw his disappearance. I saw him disappearing. I saw his existence no more. I looked forward. I smacked my royal horse. I smacked my horse again. I smacked my horse the third time. I saw something. I saw something happening. I saw my running horse. I saw my horse running. I saw my horse running faster. I saw my horse running past plenty of Sri Lankan woodlands. I saw my running horse. I saw my horse running outside the raining forest. I saw my horse running outside the Sri Lankan rain forest. I saw my horse running. I saw my horse running past Sri Lankan mountains. I saw my running horse. I saw my horse running past many Sri Lankan rivers. I rode on my running horse. I rode with my head downwards. I rode forward. I rode past plenty of Sri Lankan rain forests. I rode past plenty of Sri Lankan mountains. I rode past plenty of Sri Lankan rivers. I rode past plenty of Sri Lankan cowboys. I rode past plenty of Sri Lankan old buildings. I rode inside Sri Lankan Islands. I rode inside Cocos Keeling Islands. I rode faster. I rode past Cocos Keeling Islands. I rode past plenty of Sri Lankan Islands. I rode forward. I rode faster. I rode faster and faster. I rode faster like a warrior. I rode faster like a royal warrior. I rode faster. I rode faster like a soldier. I rode faster. I rode faster like a royal soldier. I rode farther. I rode farther and farther. I rode farther like a warrior. I rode farther. I rode farther and farther. I rode farther like a royal warrior. I rode farther. I rode farther and farther. I rode farther like a soldier. I rode farther like a royal soldier. I approached somewhere. I approached somewhere warring. I rode inside Sri Lankan war fields. I rode inside Sri Lankan battlefields. I saw plenty of dead Sri Lankan war soldiers. I saw plenty of dead Sri Lankan fighting women. I saw plenty of dead Sri Lankan fighting men. I saw plenty of dead Sri Lankan warring children. I saw plenty of collapsed Sri Lankan trenches. I saw plenty of dead Australian soldiers. I saw plenty of dead Australian fighting women. I saw plenty of dead Australian fighting men. I saw some Sri Lankan soldiers. I saw some fighting Sri Lankan soldiers. I saw some fighting Sri Lankan women. I saw some fighting Sri Lankan men. I saw some Sri Lankan children. I saw some fighting Australian soldiers. I saw some fighting Australian women. I saw some fighting Australian men. I was sitting on my royal horse. I looked forward. I saw fighting Sri Lankan soldiers. I saw fighting Australian soldiers. I saw one handsome soldier. I saw one handsome Australian soldier. I saw him fighting plenty of Sri Lankan soldiers. I saw him turning around. I saw him facing me. I saw him looking at me. I saw him holding something.

I saw him holding two weapons. I saw him holding a sword in his left hand. I saw him holding an Ak47 in his right hand. I saw him looking at me. I saw him doing something. I saw him doing something heavenly. I saw him looking at me with emotions. I saw something. I saw him doing something. I saw him dropping down his sword. I saw him dropping down his gun. I saw him dropping his weapons. I saw all the Australian soldiers. I saw them dropping down all their weapons. I saw all the Sri Lankan soldiers. I saw them dropping down all their weapons. I jumped off my royal horse. I stood upwards. I looked backwards. I saw the war veteran and his dragon. I saw my heavenly followers. I saw them behind me and my royal horse. I stood in front of the handsome Australian soldier. I saw the handsome Australian soldier. I saw him farther away from me. I looked at the handsome Australian soldier. I saw him running. I saw him running forward. I saw him running towards me. I saw him jumping higher in the sky. I saw him jumping in happiness. I saw him landing on the warring ground. I saw him landing in happiness. I saw him hugging me. I saw him speaking. I saw him speaking about something. I saw him speaking about something heavenly. I saw him saying something. I saw him saying something heavenly. I saw him shouting. I saw him shouting out loud. I saw him saying the word "FREEDOM". I heard him shouting the word "FREEDOM". I looked forward. I looked at all the Sri Lankan soldiers. I looked at all the Australian soldiers. I saw them dropping down their swords. Saw them dropping down their guns. I saw them dropping down all their weapons. I saw them shouting. I saw them shouting out loud. I saw them shouting the word "FREEDOM". I heard them shouting out loud. I heard them shouting the word "FREEDOM". I saw them running. I saw them fighting no more. I saw them running forward. I saw them running towards me and my royal horse. I saw them in front of me and my royal horse. I saw them jumping higher into the sky. I saw them jumping in happiness. I saw them landing downwards. I saw them landing onto the ground.

I saw them landing in happiness. I saw all the Australian soldiers. I saw all the Sri Lankan soldiers. I saw them all hugging me. I saw them all hugging me in happiness. I saw the handsome Australian soldier. I saw him welcoming me. I saw him welcoming me to Sri Lanka. I saw him speaking. I saw him saying something. I saw him speaking about FREEDOM. I saw him speaking about PEACE. I saw him speaking about UNITY. I saw him speaking about FIGHTING NO MORE. I gave all of them a hug. I saw someone. I saw someone appearing. I saw my heavenly lion. I saw my lion friend. I saw Leo. I saw him speaking. I saw him welcoming me to Sri Lanka. I saw him welcoming the war veteran and his dragon to Sri Lanka. I saw him congratulating me. I saw him congratulating me for completing his mission. I saw him congratulating the war veteran and his dragon. I saw him congratulating us about our journey. I saw him congratulating us on completing the mission he gave us. I saw him congratulating us for completing his mission. I saw him speaking to all the Sri Lankan and Australian soldiers. I saw him congratulating all the Sri Lankan and Australian soldiers. I saw something. I saw something happening. I saw something. I saw something strange happening. I saw something. I saw something magical happening. I saw my heavenly lion. I saw my lion friend. I saw Leo. I saw him vanishing. I saw him disappearing. I saw his existence no more. I looked forward. I looked at the Australian and Sri Lankan freedom soldiers. I waved them goodbye. I turned around. I jumped onto my royal horse. I made my journey from the Sri Lankan battlefield towards England. I am Prince Harry. I am the prince of England. This is my mysterious journey to Cocos Keeling Islands.

Written by

NICHOLAS ARMSTRONG JR